RIO GRANDE

Center Point
Large Print

**This Large Print Book carries the
Seal of Approval of N.A.V.H.**

RIO GRANDE

Curtis Bishop

CENTER POINT LARGE PRINT
THORNDIKE, MAINE

This Center Point Large Print edition is published
in the year 2016 by arrangement with
Golden West Literary Agency.

First U.S. edition: Avalon.

The text of this Large Print edition is unabridged.
In other aspects, this book may vary
from the original edition.
Printed in the United States of America
on permanent paper.
Set in 16-point Times New Roman type.

ISBN: 978-1-68324-216-1 (hardcover)
ISBN: 978-1-68324-220-8 (paperback)

Library of Congress Cataloging-in-Publication Data

Names: Bishop, Curtis, 1912–1967, author.
Title: Rio Grande / Curtis Bishop.
Description: Center Point Large Print edition. | Thorndike, Maine :
Center Point Large Print, 2016.
Identifiers: LCCN 2016042526| ISBN 9781683242161 (hardcover :
alk. paper) | ISBN 9781683242208 (pbk. : alk. paper)
Subjects: LCSH: Large type books. | GSAFD: Love stories. | Western
stories.
Classification: LCC PS3503.I7835 R56 2016 | DDC 813/.54—dc23
LC record available at https://lccn.loc.gov/2016042526

to *Clarence Long*
the greatest domino player
in the world

Author's Note:

The author has borrowed heavily from history to concoct this story of the Texas *monte* or *brasada*, where the heritage of the American cattleman was born.

The entire military action is closely linked with fact. Woll's capture of San Antonio, Somervell's baffling management of a much-publicized invasion, the assault on Mier, and the grim lottery of Salado—such events actually occurred, and very much as pictured here.

Some liberty is taken with the legendary priest of the border, Father Andrew Muldoon. But let any reader who resents such a fictional role for a religious figure consider that Muldoon arranged William H. Wharton's escape from a Matamoros prison very much as he liberated Joel in this tale.

Sam Walker, Jack Hays, Ewen Cameron, Big Foot Wallace, Ben McCulloch, and Bill Thompson were real men, and are not exaggerated in these pages. Walker, Thompson, and two other Texians escaped from Molino del Ray exactly as depicted.

Just about all the author has done, in fact, is to weave the make-believe romance of Joel Howard and Consuela O'Rourke into a little-known chapter of American history. If they seem to fit it, I am very pleased.

Chapter One

Sam Walker insisted that Joel accept the five-shooters.

"You've earned 'em, bucko. You've saved old Sam's hide twice. Besides, I can hustle another pair."

Joel hesitated. He wasn't too sure that Walker could replace the heavy-barreled Colt revolvers. Only the Texas Rangers boasted such weapons in 1842. Their manufacturer in New York had gone out of business.

"Now, don't gimme any sass," snapped Sam. "I want you to have 'em."

Joel's face lit up. He sure would take them since Sam insisted. He strapped the guns around his lean middle. Their pouches must hang lower; he was a taller man than Walker. But that could wait.

Sam Walker was quitting Ewen Cameron's brush-popping crew. Such business, he said, was too rough for him. Twice he had narrowly escaped death as his riata missed and outraged bulls charged him. He hoped he would never see an ugly, savage ladino again, he declared. He was heading back to the rangers where he ran normal risks like Comanches and Mexican banditos.

Joel fondled the pistols. "I'm sure obliged, Sam," he said huskily. "I can't tell you how obliged I am."

"No call to," Sam said gruffly. He held out his hand. "Lemme know if you ever want to sign up with us, bucko. You'd make Jack a good hand."

By Jack he meant Major Jack Hays, commander of the scout troop known as the rangers. The Republic of Texas boasted no other regular military force. There were volunteer companies, minutemen. Ewen Cameron held a captain's rank in this force. But the rangers bore the brunt of fighting off Comanches and watching for another invasion from Mexico.

"I'd like to, Sam," said Joel. "But I'm making good money with Ewen. And I want to fix up my place this winter."

"Sure," nodded Sam. "You're getting ahead." He had learned quite a bit about twenty-year-old Joel Howard in this past month. The gangling Joel was Cameron's best cattle hand, and earned the biggest split when the ladinos were delivered at Goliad. Joel owned a thousand acres of brush-land along the Medina River and aspired to operate his own rancho.

"You sure don't do bad," repeated Sam. "Well, I'll mosey, bucko. Look me up if you ever want to do some riding and shooting."

Joel promised. He watched Walker until he was

out of sight and then squatted Indian-fashion to gloat over his pistols. He could use them already; Walker had taught him. And Sam knew more about these five-shooters than their inventor. Walker had traveled all the way to New York to show Samuel Colt how the revolvers could be adapted for use on horseback. A trigger guard, a heavier hammer and Mr. Colt had himself a gun! The Texas Republic bought his entire stock and in gratitude the inventor called his revamped weapon the "Walker Model."

Joel tried a few shots, then remounted his chestnut mustang and returned to the grind. Ewen Cameron paid his workers by the head, not the day. Every ladino prodded into the trap meant two dollars for its captor. Ewen had organized these wild cattle hunts into a profitable business. He financed the expeditions and attended to the selling. His hands received pay according to tally. Joel had earned seventy dollars in his very first month, which had ruined him for farming, especially share-cropping. Now he averaged twice as much as in the first month.

He lassoed another wild steer, then quit for the day. Ewen's other hands were already in camp and wolfing down beans, dried fruit, roasted venison and sourdough bread. The Scot fed his crews well, which was one of several reasons why he could keep operating.

Joel ate swiftly. He had reddish-brown hair and

a strong aversion to either hat or cap. He sat bare-headed now, his blue eyes studying his hardcase companions. He liked most of these unkempt, coarse-speaking men, but not Jared Applegate and Pierre Boulain. Both were new men, and Joel sensed that Ewen did not care for them, either. Jared was a troublemaker and Boulain let his dark-featured bullnecked friend call every turn.

"I see Walker give you his guns," said Applegate.

Joel nodded.

"Don't put too much store by 'em," Jared advised. "The right hombre will cram 'em down your throat if you get too gay."

Joel said nothing. He meant to avoid trouble with Applegate if he could. But the bullnecked man's attitude got harder and harder to take.

No crisis came now. Instead, came Indians out of the brush, a score of brownskinned big-hatted men on wiry ponies. The brushpoppers were caught off guard. Several reached for their rifles and Joel drew one of the repeating revolvers. But Ewen stopped any show of resistance. The Indian leader swung down from his pony and came slowly toward the men. Obviously, he meant no harm.

He was a thin, stooped man whose catlike walk belied his white hair and flowing mustaches. He wore a straw sombrero pushed back on his head, a beaded sleeveless shirt with leather gauntlets reaching up to his elbows. He carried a short-handled whip in his right hand, his only weapon. The other Indians boasted muskets, holding them loosely as they sat their horses stolidly, their dark bright eyes watching their *jefe*.

The Indian studied Cameron a moment, then demanded: "*Quien Estan?*"

Ewen spoke faltering Spanish. The vaquero let loose a spirited tirade. When the Scot protested, the white-mustached Indian shook his head firmly.

"What's it all about, Ewen?" demanded Applegate.

Ewen turned to his crew. "He calls himself the *caporal* for Carlos Garza. We are on Garza land, he says. He will allow no more cattle hunting without this Don Carlos' permission."

Joel listened in silence. They had never encountered this sort of resistance before. But, he realized, this was their first hunt south of the Nueces River. They were in virgin territory as far as brushpoppers were concerned.

"Tell him we'll trap cattle where we danged please," snapped Jared.

A rifle clicked behind Joel. The natives sensed the meaning of these hostile words.

"We'll have no trouble," Ewen ordered in his strong Scotch accent.

The Scot turned back to the *caporal*. More talk followed. The aged Indian seemed partially reassured; his white head bobbed again and again. He pointed upstream with his whip. Then he swung up on his mustang and led his vaqueros away without another word or gesture. The Indians melted into the *monte* as suddenly as they had appeared.

"We must get the bigwig's permission," Ewen explained to his crew.

"And what if this Don so-and-so tells us to git?" The question came from Applegate. Who else, thought Joel? Only Jared and his hulking French companion questioned Cameron's authority.

"Then we will get," the Scot said calmly. "This land belongs to Carlos Garza under Texas law. We have always operated under the law and we will. I shall ask this Don Carlos' permission to hunt this creek. If he turns us down—"

Ewen shrugged his shoulders. His meaning was clear. He would not dispute the authority of a Spanish *proprietor* to order them off his land.

The brushpoppers settled back to await the verdict. Joel passed away the time splicing two riatas into one. Ewen rode back with the announcement that Don Carlos would not discuss the business until the next day.

"There is a fiesta tonight," the Scot explained,

14

"in honor of Father Andrew Muldoon. Our business must wait."

"You mean you're cowtailing to this greaser?" demanded Applegate.

"I am respecting his rights of ownership," Ewen said. "He received us friendly enough. We are invited to the fiesta and *baille*."

"Now, ain't that plumb sweet!" sneered Jared.

"It shore is," spoke up Waldo Prewitt. He was a lanky man in his early thirties with a zest for human companionship. "And I shore aim to take him up. You ain't seen nuthing until you watch old Prewitt cut didoes with pretty *senoritas*."

Cameron smiled faintly. "It would be good if we went," he said. "These people go all out to honor their priest. But every man on his best behavior, mind you. We want to make friends with these people, not start trouble."

"Yippee," yelped Curly Wilkins. "Who's for the *baille*? You, Joel, old son?"

Joel hesitated, then nodded eagerly. For three years now he had heard glowing reports of Mexican *bailles*. The Texians might loathe Santa Anna and hold the average native in contempt, but they enjoyed Mexican dances.

"If I string along," Joel said, "will you kinda show me what to do?"

"Like what?"

"Oh, you know. How to ask a *senorita* to dance. Things like that."

"Shucks," said Curly with a grin, "there ain't no wrong way. Just put on your Sunday-go-to-meeting clothes and cut loose."

Cameron's company worked feverishly with razors, combs and brushes. They had brought extra garments in the wagon; even Joel had a suit. It wasn't much, he thought glumly—a black broadcloth suit bought in 1839. Then he had been only a farm hand and the choice had pleased him. Now it was no good at all. A would-be *caballero* wearing such a dull costume! Curly boasted a purple shirt and bright silk kerchief. Waldo put on a checkered shirt and cream-colored vest with pearl buttons.

Only Applegate and Boulain showed no enthusiasm. "You pea-pickers are heading for a letdown," said Jared. He had seen these greaser pueblos make a fuss over visiting padres, he said. Once he'd watched a mass wedding service performed by this same Father Muldoon.

"Nuthing wrong with that," Prewitt objected. "Texians get hitched about the same way. A justice of the peace can do it if there ain't a preacher around."

"Father Muldoon," put in Ewen, "was a familiar figure in Austin's colonies. And well-regarded, too."

"Not by me," snapped Jared.

Curly was ready now and he and Joel rode off together.

16

"That Jared oughta stay in camp," Curly said. "He'll stir up trouble as sure as you're born."

Joel agreed.

Then they were at the native settlement and Joel forgot about Applegate in the excitement of his first fiesta. Curly seemed to know what to do and Joel followed behind his partner like a wide-eyed, trusting dog. First they ate—*tortillas* rolled up and dipped into pots of brown beans, mutton and chile, round yellow cheese sliced thin, the sweetest honey Joel had ever tasted. The Mexicans flocked around them in friendly curiosity and Joel wished he knew the words to reassure them of his appreciation. Curly did, and these brown-featured people, young and old alike, smiled broadly at everything he said.

Their appetites sated, Curly led the way to the *baille*. Joel watched enviously as Wilkins and Waldo quickly appropriated *ninas* and started to dance. There seemed to be more women than men, he mused. The women without partners sat on benches around the tile floor. Joel drank in their colorful and varied costumes. Here were bare legs and legs in silk stockings. Young and old alike made play with their best *mantillas*. Gold and silver ornaments dangled from their wrists. Babies lay in sleeping bundles on the floor while their mothers swayed to the music of a lone fiddler. Candles all around the room cast a rich, elusive light.

"Joel," said Ewen suddenly at his elbow, "I want you to meet Father Muldoon."

Joel hesitated. It was his first meeting with a priest; he wasn't sure whether to offer his hand or not; Father Muldoon settled his doubt with a quick, firm handshake. He was a short, stocky man with friendly blue eyes.

"Father Muldoon will intercede for us with Don Carlos," Ewen explained.

"I'll be happy to do so," said the priest. "I never miss a chance to help build friendly relations between our two peoples."

Father Muldoon touched Joel's arms. "But don't waste your time, my young friend. The dance is warming up, and I'm sure some of our *senoritas* have already sized you up. They have sharp eyes for big handsome *Yanquis*, especially redheads."

He and Ewen walked away. Joel slowly went inside. He saw Curly at once, dancing with a barelegged red-skirted girl. Curly came up to Joel as the music stopped.

"There's a lonesome old lobo," Wilkins sang out. "Grab a *nina*, son, and get going."

Joel shook his head. He was trying to get up the nerve to join in the frolic but he wasn't ready.

"You're scared," jeered Curly. "Plumb scared. Nothing to it, hoss. Pick out your chicken and I'll do your asking."

Joel's eyes swept the row of women and girls

and settled on a *senorita* sitting beside a plump matron.

"That one."

Curly shook his head. "She's *rico*."

"What's that?"

"Upper class."

Joel studied the girl again. She wore a white skirt embroidered with red and yellow flowers, a silk bodice trimmed with lace, and a red and black *mantilla.* A paper rose was fastened in her heavy black hair.

"You said you'd ask," Joel grinned. "Now who's yellow?"

Curly grinned. "All right, you danged fool. Come on."

He pulled Joel toward the *senorita* in the white skirt. Bowing and gesturing, he talked glibly in a mixture of Spanish and English. The next thing Joel knew, the girl was holding out bare, silverbound arms. And the music was starting. Joel held her gingerly; she was so soft and dainty and sweet-smelling that he was almost afraid to touch her.

Carefully he began to move. She was tall; his mouth was close against her ear. After a few gliding steps, Joel realized he was not dancing so badly. At least, he hadn't stumbled or caught his foot in her skirts.

"*Hablo Espanol, senor?*" she asked softly.

"No," Joel said regretfully.

"Then speak English, sir," she said lightly. "I am familiar with your tongue."

Joel gulped. "You sure are."

"You are one of *Senor* Cameron's vaqueros?"

"Not exactly," Joel said. "I'm a ladino hunter, all right. But with us every man is his own man."

Her dark eyes shone. "I was sure of that," she said. "I did not think you could be anyone else's man."

All too soon the music stopped. Joel released her and she stepped back, but did not move toward her seat by the wall. Obviously she was waiting for him to say more.

"I'm sure much obliged, ma'am," Joel managed to mutter. "You were mighty nice to put up with me." He grinned sheepishly. "That's the first time I ever danced—like that."

Her eyebrows went up. "How did you dance with the others, *senor*?"

"Well," he explained, "we sort of cavort. Do a lot of stomping around."

She nodded. She had watched the others and knew just what he meant.

"I'm glad you didn't stomp. I'd much rather dance."

Just then a Mexican in purple velvet came quickly to her side and started speaking rapidly. Joel scowled. There was no doubting that this young don was reprimanding her for dancing with a gringo. No doubting either that this *senorita* did not care for his reproachful attitude. She answered rather sharply. Joel guessed that she told *Senor* Purple Suit to attend to his own knitting. With a toss of her dark head, she turned back to Joel.

"You didn't tell me your name, *senor*."

"No, ma'am. It's Joel—Joel Howard."

"Joel?" She pronounced it. "Ho-el."

"Yes, ma'am."

A dimple appeared in each of her cheeks. Never before had she even thought of introducing herself to a young man, but now she did just that. "I'm Consuela O'Rourke," she said. "Don Carlos is my grandfather."

Joel winced. Curly had warned him that she was *rico*, that she might even belong to the Garza family. But her name—O'Rourke? She saw and understood his confusion.

"My father was Irish," she explained. Then, as he still wondered, she added, "It isn't too uncommon, *senor*. More than one Irishman took service in the New World with the King of Spain."

The don standing beside her was growing more and more impatient. Consuela's eyes twinkled mischievously. "*Senor* Howard," she said sweetly, "let me present Captain Manuel Canales."

The captain bowed stiffly. Joel nodded an acknowledgement of the introduction.

"Captain Canales," Consuela added, "is somewhat of a hero in our country, *senor.* No doubt you have heard of his uncle, General Antonio Canales."

Joel scowled. Indeed he had. General Canales had spearheaded the unhappy effort to form the northern provinces of Mexico into a separate republic. Ewen Cameron had played some part in this intrigue and was still bitter about it.

"I have heard of General Canales," Joel said slowly. The captain's open hostility relieved Joel's self-consciousness. He knew how to deal with this attitude. Consuela O'Rourke, the granddaughter of Don Carlos, could fluster him, but not this cold-eyed, haughty, foppish Mexican officer. Joel studied Captain Canales with mild contempt. A Mexican captain—what did he amount to? He could not fight, and he did not work. Canales' eyes flashed as he sensed the thoughts of this strapping, copper-haired Texian. The Mexican's hand went to the hilt of his dress sword.

Joel turned back to Consuela. Thanks to this Captain Canales he was no longer tongue-tied.

"I enjoyed the dance, *senorita*," he said. "May I look forward to another?"

Her dark eyes shone and her lips parted, but she shook her head. "No," she said gently but firmly. "I have been most improper as it is. Enjoy yourself with another partner, *Senor* Joel."

She took Canales' arm and walked back to her seat. Curly Wilkins rushed up.

"Boy, you pulled it off," he grinned. "I didn't figure you had the nerve. Come on, I'll get another *nina* for you."

Joel shook his head. He was not interested in dancing with anyone else, not now. No other girl here held a candle to Consuela O'Rourke. Probably no one anywhere did.

"Nope," he said. "I'm going outside for some air. I need it—after her."

Chapter Two

Joel watched the *baille* for a while, then decided that he had had enough. Anything else that happened now would be a letdown. He sighed. She had certainly thrown him for a loop. One look had done it, too, one look followed by a flash of her dark eyes and a quick smile. And she realized it. The teasing minx—speaking Spanish first, then switching to flawless English.

He moved toward his horse, hobbled a hundred yards away from the cluster of *jacals*. As he was bridling his pony he heard curses ahead of him and recognized Applegate's voice.

"All right, you pot-bellied padre," he heard Jared say. "Start your crow-hopping."

Joel listened more closely.

"I mean it, Padre. You'll put on a show or we'll flay your hide to ribbons."

Joel hurried toward the commotion. He came into a small clearing and saw that Applegate, Boulain and two others had Father Muldoon in their power. Jared and Pierre held quirts while the Frenchman also brandished a pistol.

The padre faced his tormentors fearlessly. He was pale, but unafraid.

"You may use that quirt all you wish," the priest said, "but you cannot force me to demean my habit."

"Habit!" sneered Jared. "You priests don't fool me. You're spies for the greasers, that's all."

Joel licked his lips, then stepped forward quickly. "What's going on?" he demanded.

"A little show, that's all," Applegate told him. "The padre here is gonna put it on for us. He's gonna do a little jig for us out here in the moonlight. Cute, ain't it?"

"No," Joel said coldly. "Ewen won't stand for it and you know it."

"Ewen ain't here," snapped Jared.

"But I am."

Jared crouched slightly and squinted at Joel. "You aim to stop me?"

"I sure do," Joel said. "Father Muldoon wants to be our friend."

"Reckon you're some coon, ain't you?" sneered Jared. "Ewen's pet, too. Well, I ain't treed a young frisky coon in quite a spell. You're my pigeon, buckie boy."

Joel paled slightly as Jared slowly circled him. He had no intention of backing down, but at the same time he realized what he was up against. Why doubt how Jared would fight? Nothing barred. Joel let him come closer without making any show of resistance. Let Jared relax his guard, be overeager—there he came! Joel hit Applegate squarely in the stomach. The big man grunted and staggered backward and Joel drove at the stocky man with both hands. He hooked one arm

25

around Jared's neck, flipped an ankle behind him and pummeled Applegate's dark face. As he pushed Jared backward he hooked his left lbow into the other man's nose.

Jared landed heavily but bounced right back up, crowing as if this swift brutal bit of punishment had not hurt him at all. He rushed at Joel but the younger man sidestepped and drove for Jared's hips. He caught Applegate above the knees and lifted him free of the ground, then slammed him down heavily. But instead of falling on his man, Joel leaped back. The squat Jared fell like a cat, with both boots lashing upward. It was never very hard to get Applegate down. But those who tried to pin him to the ground usually carried the scars a long time afterward.

Missing his kick, Jared rolled to his feet. Joel tried to hit him solidly as he came off the ground but overswung. Even rising, Jared could hit like a mule. Joel felt his mouth ripped open; the impact sent Joel spinning and a red sea surged before his eyes. For an instant he felt cold, paralyzing fear. Lordee, what a powerful brute! In one quick blow Jared had more than made up for all the times Joel had hit him.

Applegate came after him hard. Joel feinted, falling away, then came into Jared backward and low. Fists thudded down on his head and shoulders but he caught a knee and upended

Jared again. He hooked his elbow into Jared's snarling mouth and brought up his knee against the squat man's windpipe. Then Joel was up again with a handful of dirt. Hurling it into Jared's eyes, he drove forward, butting with his head.

Applegate fell backward, hurt now. The way he crouched, with one hand behind him, warned Joel. Jared had his knife. Joel dived in quickly, beating the other's lunge. He hit with his right hand, battering Jared's mouth. He seized Jared's shoulder and spun the bullnecked man around. He caught Jared's right hand and jerked it upward as he drove his knee into the small of his adversary's back.

"Drop it," he panted.

Jared snarled a curse. Joel drove his knee again and again into Applegate's ribs and spine. His breath came shorter. Finally he let the bowie drop to the ground. But, as Joel relaxed his hold, Jared broke free and dived for the weapon. Joel instantly swung his knee into the stumbling man's face and sent him sprawling, then jumped and landed with both feet on Jared's right hand. His breath coming in wheezy jerks, he stepped back. That hand would not wield a knife for a long time, if it ever did again.

Now Joel realized that a crowd had gathered for this brutal finish. Cameron's company was watching to a man, and many of the *pelandos* as well. Even a few women were there staring.

And, as his bloodshot eyes circled the crowd defiantly, Joel saw the Mexican officer, Manuel Canales.

Ewen stepped to Joel's side and caught his shoulder.

"What started this, lad?" the Scot demanded.

Joel shook his head. He couldn't talk, not yet. He gestured to Father Muldoon.

"The young man was protecting me, Mr. Cameron," explained the priest. "Some of your men tried to make sport with me."

"What were they doing?"

Father Muldoon explained. Ewen glared around him. Applegate lay cursing on the ground; Boulain and the others had disappeared.

"I'm sorry, Father," said Cameron. "I'll settle with these scoundrels. Curly, take Applegate to the wagon. Bandage up his hand as best you can and send him packing."

The Scot turned back to the priest. "I suppose there's no way we can keep these things from happening," he said awkwardly. "We're a pretty rowdy lot."

"Do not apologize, Mr. Cameron. Joel has convinced me again that there are fine men in Texas as well as everywhere else." He took the trembling youth's arm. "I have a *jacal* nearby for my own use. Don Carlos built it for me, for I'm never comfortable in the luxury of a hacienda. I'll take Joel and doctor his cuts and bruises.

And I suggest that you bring him to see Don Carlos tomorrow. I know Don Carlos will appreciate what he has done."

The priest turned to the awed spectators. "The rest of you go back to the *baille*. We mustn't let this unpleasantness spoil the fiesta."

Chapter Three

The sunrise chorus brought Consuela O'Rourke wide awake. Birds in the *huisaches* chirped noisily, especially the bluejays. Downstairs the Indian women were stirring, their huaraches scuffling across the tiles. She heard the creak of a *carreta*; there was no muffling the sound of the wooden wheels.

Consuela called for her chocolate, and Maria came running. Consuela sipped the sweet, thick liquid, smiling as she recalled the events of last night. How curious Manuel Canales had been! And how vexed her grandfather, until she had cajoled him back into a good humor! Until, too, Don Carlos had heard how the copper-haired *Yanqui* had defended Father Muldoon. That had made a great difference. Her grandfather usually obeyed the priest with astonishing meekness. Nobody else could influence him, except Consuela, and then only about small things. Don Carlos lived in the past, as Manuel was learning. Consuela's eyes danced. Poor Manuel! He was so sure that his military assignment would bring him land and wealth and the right to marry Don Carlos' granddaughter. Manuel had hoped to get money from Don Carlos for

Santa Anna's scheme to reconquer Texas. So far the *proprietor* hadn't said yea or nay.

Consuela rose lazily. Maria poured water into a silver bowl for her mistress to wash. The Indian woman moved cautiously, not wishing to disturb Consuela's absorption. The girl was in a kind of daydream, wishing that she had seen the fight. The copper-haired *Yanqui* had stomped the other's hand. Both *Yanquis,* said her informants, were *muy forte.* The pueblo would talk about that fight for a long time.

Her toilette made, Consuela hurried down to breakfast. She ate heartily, noticing nothing unusual about her grandfather's silence. It was his way to brood over small decisions.

"I have decided," Don Carlos finally announced, "to let the *Yanquis* hunt on my land. I saw no good coming out of it at first. But maybe Father Muldoon is right and we should try to be friendly with them."

Consuela's eyes danced. She approved of that.

"Apparently," continued her grandfather in that same brooding manner, "the *Yanquis* realize some value from wild cattle. I don't see how. We use it only for making chile.

"They are coming here this morning," he added as an afterthought. "This *Senor* Howard and the *Yanqui caporal, Senor* Cameron."

Consuela gasped. The red-haired *Yanqui* coming here!

"How soon?" she asked faintly.

"Oh, some time this morning. It does not matter." Consuela looked at her grandfather disgustedly. It *did* matter.

"Will I see them?"

Don Carlos frowned. It was not the usual thing. The *Yanquis* were coming on business, not as guests. Then he yielded to the pleading in his granddaughter's eyes. "If you like," he said reluctantly. "You may receive them in the *sala.*"

The hacienda filled Joel with awe. He had never seen anything like it before. Lagging behind Ewen, he studied every detail closely. The spring which formed Agua Dulce Creek bubbled up out of a valley, overflowing in a deep clear pool. Indian women on its banks stopped their washing to stare curiously at the two *Yanquis.* The first Garza had built this two-winged adobe house to utilize the shade of *huisaches* and willows, and to catch every breath of breeze from the southeast. Behind the sprawling red-roofed structure clustered the *jacals*, farther on the maze of corrals and cribs. Sheep fed everywhere and Joel saw, for his first time, *acequias* irrigating lush orchards and gardens.

Mozos came running to take their horses and Joel reluctantly followed Ewen to the brass-trimmed door of the big house. He wanted to learn more about the irrigation of this valley. He might adapt some of these ideas to his own land eventually. He owned a valley, too, but he had built his cabin on a wooded rise.

Then they were facing Don Carlos, and Joel looked closely at this courtly, dignified man who owned half a million acres of land. He saw a slight but erect man in his early sixties, heard a cultured voice welcome them to his hacienda. "My house is yours," Don Carlos said simply. Such an interior, too—huge rooms with high ceilings and tiled floors, frescoed walls, gleaming candelabra. The awed Joel sank into a deep chair and accepted wine in a thin glass tumbler.

For a few moments he listened closely to the talk between Ewen and Don Carlos. Judging by their expressions and the tone of their voices, Don Carlos was willing for the gringos to trap along the creek. Then Joel's attention wandered to other things. He noted the woven rugs scattered about and the tapestries which covered the walls halfway to the ceiling. He found himself wondering what revenues Don Carlos realized from his far-flung estates. If the Spaniard considered ladinos worthless, then what did he sell or trade?

"Joel, Don Carlos is speaking to you."

He started and stammered his apologies.

"I want to commend your protection of Father Muldoon," said the Spaniard. "It was a

33

dastardly thing to so maltreat a worthy man of God."

"That bunch are bad customers," Joel said. "The rest of us are glad Ewen sent 'em packing."

He suddenly realized he should have referred to the Scot as Mister Cameron. He had almost forgotten formality in these last few years.

"None of them are really Texians," Ewen told Don Carlos. "Boulain is French. The Republic of Texas is becoming a polyglot of peoples."

"Apparently," agreed the *proprietor.* Plainly he disapproved. The entrance of Canales stopped talk momentarily. He was as carefully dressed as he had been the night before, in a velveteen waistcoast and ruffled shirt and tight-fitting breeches. His manner was gently polite, but Joel made mental note of his cold and shifty eyes. Here was the type of Spaniard, he mused, that Ewen had warned him about, suave but treacherous.

"I have heard of Captain Cameron," Manuel said after his introduction to the Scot. "I believe you were associated with my uncle."

The tall Scot did not evade issues. "Only for a time," he said curtly. "I withdrew when the Republic of the Rio Grande became a spring-board for Santa Anna's return to power."

"Necessity always enters into politics," Manuel said smoothly. "Lopez de Santa Anna may have his faults, but he is good for my country as a whole."

"*Your* country?" Cameron said. "Then you are in Texas as a visitor?"

Canales showed a thin smile. "Yes and no, *senor.* Texas claims the territory between the Nueces and the Rio Grande. But I know of no world power which has recognized that claim."

"That will come," Ewen said shortly. Joel's eyes twinkled. If this suave officer wanted an argument, he could have one. Ewen Cameron never missed an opportunity to demonstrate his fervent loyalty to his adopted country. The Scot strongly championed President Mirabeau B. Lamar's aggressive policies of cxpansion.

Don Carlos rose, as if to forestall a possible disagreement.

"My granddaughter has asked to see you," he told Joel. "She wants to voice her own thanks for your aid to Father Muldoon. This way, if you will."

Joel's face crimsoned, but he had no intention of holding back. All the way to the Garza hacienda he had wondered if he would see her. Curly Wilkins had predicted that he would not. According to Curly these dons held their wives and daughters virtual prisoners in upstairs bed-rooms.

But there she sat in the *sala*, needle and embroidery piece in her hand, a cup of chocolate by her side. The long room was cool and dark; she and her *duenna* needed candles for their sewing. Their light was multiplied in mirrors with gilt frames. On the walls hung bright pictures of saints and cardinals with folded hands. The floor was softened with a coarse dark woolen carpet and lamb's-wool rugs washed fleecy white. A tiny shrine with a wooden figure of Jesus filled one corner of the room.

The atmosphere touched Joel, who had not attended a religious rite of any kind in four years. Was this some kind of a sanctuary?

Consuela looked up at him with a smile.

"*Buenas dias, Senor* Ho-el," she said.

"*Buenas dias,*" he answered awkwardly.

After a word to his granddaughter, Don Carlos returned to his other guest. Consuela sat on a wide bench, her impassive *duenna* a few feet away in a chair.

"Will you sit down, *senor*?" she asked after a moment.

He hesitated, then gingerly took a seat on the bench. A smile lurked about the corners of Consuela's lips. How shy he was, how uncertain of what to do or say! It didn't seem possible that he could be transformed into a furious demon of a man. Yet, studying him from under her eyebrows, she saw evidences of strength. His embarrassment did not hide the firm cut of his chin nor the tightness of his mouth. He was

36

timid and ill at ease, but he was not afraid. Her pulse quickened as she realized that this tall *Yanqui* was not the least bit afraid of her. Manuel was, usually, and was never bold except with his eyes.

"You may speak English, *senor*," Consuela said chidingly. "I learned it in childhood."

Joel stirred. "Truth is," he finally blurted out, "I can't think of anything to say."

Consuela dropped her head to hide her smile. It was impossible to keep from teasing him. "Am I so unattractive, then?" she murmured. "Some young men claim I inspire them to pretty speeches."

She was glad that her *duenna* did not understand English. She would not want such boldness reported to her grandfather.

"I'm no hand at pretty speeches," Joel said regretfully. "Truth is," he added, "I don't know much about courting girls."

Consuela's slim shoulders trembled with her inward pleasure. She had not realized that any man could be so refreshingly naive.

"You aren't courting me, *senor*," she said softly. "You can't—not without my grandfather's permission."

"And I don't reckon there's a chance of getting that."

He spoke for his own benefit, not hers. He was telling himself, almost under his breath, that he had better get any romantic notions out of his thick head. She was *rico*.

"Small chance," Consuela agreed. "My grandfather carefully considers my prospective suitors."

She did not explain the reason for such caution, that Don Carlos had never reconciled himself completely to his daughter's marriage to Thomas O'Rourke, a handsome, adventurous Irishman who had scoffed at the customs of the Garzas and their kind. Garza had made a pretense of accepting his son-in-law but never succeeded in putting his prejudices entirely aside. He wanted Consuela to marry a highborn Spanish *proprietor* like himself.

Joel took out his kerchief and wiped his forehead. He was cutting a sorry figure, and he knew it. The surroundings bothered him. The shrine and the pictures of holy men made light conversation seem out of place. This room reminded him of a church, and he had been taught not to talk in church.

He pointed to the outside door. "Could we go out on the patio and talk?" he asked.

Consuela looked mischievously at her *duenna*, then nodded. "Of course," she agreed, leading him through the door.

Donna Theresa followed obediently.

"Does she have to tag along?" Joel asked.

"Of course, *Senor* Howard," the girl said meekly. "It is our custom."

38

"Hanged if I like it," Joel said disgustedly. "Nothing wrong with a fellow taking a girl for a walk, is there?"

"No," Consuela agreed. "But customs are customs, *senor*. And I am a most dutiful grand-daughter."

He looked at her quickly. The frank challenge in his eyes was too much for Consuela's self-control. She could not suppress a soft giggle. Slowly a smile spread across Joel's features.

"That's what I figgered," he said. "You've got fire—and vinegar, too. I'll bet you can wrap Don Carlos around your little finger."

"*Senor*," she reproved him, "you do not tell a young lady she is filled with vinegar."

But Consuela had awed him for the last time—in such a way, at least. "Probably some of the devil, too," he said with a shrug. He pointed toward the sheep feeding by the spring pool. "Your granddad takes care of his sheep. Doesn't he give a hoot about cattle?"

"A hoot? I don't understand, *senor*."

"Doesn't he tame 'em, fatten 'em?"

"Some. But we don't value cattle too highly, *senor*. Why should we? They are here—every-where around us."

Joel nodded. "And horses, too. Running around everywhere."

"But we raise horses," she objected. "Pure

39

Arabian. My grandfather has sold horses in Monterey and Saltilla."

"Blooded stock. Too much trouble to handle. No good going after ladinos."

Consuela smiled. "We do not hunt wild cattle, *senor*. You *Yanquis* do that."

"Good money in it." Joel leaned forward, still staring over the valley. "But I could learn a lot from your grandfather about corrals and cribs. I haven't built any improvements on my land yet. Just the start of a cabin and about a hundred cattle foraging for themselves. I oughta have some sheep, too, and a few of those milch goats." He grinned ruefully. "There's a heck of a lot I haven't even started to do yet."

"You have a rancho, *senor*?" Consuela asked softly, looking at him wonderingly. She was not sure she understood all he was saying. She had never before heard anyone discuss cribs and cattle and corrals as if they were really important.

"I reckon," Joel said. "Nothing like your place. Just four sections, not even a league." He looked down, twisting his big hands. "You see, I didn't inherit anything, *senorita*," he explained. "I came to Texas with just the clothes on my back. My land, I got it buying headrights for little or nothing. From army veterans mostly, some of 'em got theirs for fighting at San

Jacinto." His voice faltered. "Reckon I shouldn't have mentioned that."

"Why not, *senor*?"

"Well, you're Spanish, or your granddad is. I reckon it's a sore subject."

"No," said Consuela, more thoughtful than usual. "At least I don't think so. My grandfather has never admired Lopez de Santa Anna. And that's what the revolution was about, wasn't it? The Texians threw off Santa Anna's yoke."

"Yes, ma'am," said Joel. "That's how it started anyhow." He saw no use in adding that Texian hostility now extended to all Mexican people, to the whole country of Mexico. Most Texians wanted their republic to become a part of the United States as one or several states. Though not too concerned with political philosophies, Joel shared that desire. He had come to Texas believing that he was helping to move America's frontier west-ward.

Just then Don Carlos called out rather sharply; Consuela gathered up her sewing and rose to her feet.

"I must go, *senor*," she said. "My grandfather thinks we have been alone long enough."

"Gosh, we haven't been alone," protested Joel, nodding to the imperturbable *duenna*. "And I was just getting warmed up."

Consuela gnawed her lower lip uncertainly. She wanted to see this tall gringo again, to hear more of his strange, rambling talk. She had discovered in these last few minutes that he had a quiet self-confidence which she had not observed in any other man. And there was no doubting the challenge in his eyes and his tilted chin.

"There is a back patio," she whispered. "My grandfather retires early. My *duenna*, too. I might be there—tonight."

"I will be there," Joel said quickly.

"Hush," Consuela warned him softly. Her voice rose. "Let me thank you again for rescuing Father Muldoon, *Senor* Howard."

She turned and swept by her grandfather and Manuel Canales. Nothing in her expression showed that she had agreed to a secret tryst with the tall *Yanqui*.

Chapter Four

Or did Manuel Canales sense something? He was a jealous man; now he studied Joel Howard with cold, hostile eyes. For two years Canales had wooed Don Carlos' granddaughter. Now his moment was almost at hand, when he could formally ask for her as a wife. The arrival of these *Yanquis* was quite disturbing to the Mexican captain. In the first place, they had interrupted his efforts to get financial help for Santa Anna's proposed invasion. And now this red-haired *Yanqui* had made a shocking impression on Consuela.

Was the *Yanqui* worth worrying about? He shouldn't be, not a tall, ungainly foreigner in ill-fitting clothes who chased after wild cattle for a living! But Manuel couldn't forget that Consuela's mother had married a foreigner despite Don Carlos' disapproval. Canales followed Ewen and Joel out of the house.

"A word with you, *Senor* Howard," he said curtly.

"Shoot," agreed Joel, following Canales a short distance away.

"It concerns the *Senorita* Consuela. She was most gracious to you this morning. She is grateful for your aid to Father Muldoon. But do not presume further. It would be unwise of you to see her again."

43

Joel's grin formed slowly. This Spaniard was jealous of him! Had he really made that much of an impression on Consuela O'Rourke? It was a thrilling thought.

"That will be up to the *senorita*," Joel said calmly.

Manuel's eyes blazed. *Yanquis*—did they have no respect for convention?

"I have warned you, *Senor* Howard," he said coldly. "Now I hope we do not meet again."

He turned and strode into the hacienda. Joel looked after him with a grin. He didn't fear Canales or any other Spaniard. The talk he had heard was that one Texian could whip ten Mexicans.

"Well," said Ewen as Joel rejoined him, "you had quite a conversation."

"Yep," said Joel with a grin. He hesitated, then satisfied Ewen's curiosity. "He warned me to steer clear of *Senorita* O'Rourke."

The Scot did not smile back; instead, he said gravely, "I was preparing to do the same. Lad, the *ninas* in a pueblo are one thing, a highborn *senorita* another. I've done some inquiring about Don Carlos. He's neither for Santa Anna or against him. The Garzas have never relinquished any of their original rights as *proprietors*. Their vaqueros go armed to the teeth and can make mince-meat of banditos. He could attack us with a hundred natives if he were a mind to. And he will—if you aren't careful about his granddaughter."

Joel's eyes danced. Ewen Cameron, too! Golly, Joel could hardly believe it. She had been friendly, yes. She had teased him, too. Did that mean what Canales and Cameron seemed to think? What would the Mexican captain and the Scot think if they knew about her half-promise to meet him on the back patio tonight? He had no intention of telling Ewen. The Scot would think Joel a crazy fool to risk the rage of a *proprietor* who could command a hundred vaqueros. Joel smiled. It would make no difference if Don Carlos could call out a thousand armed men.

Less than a mile from the hacienda they met Father Muldoon plodding along on his small mule. Ewen tried to voice his thanks for the padre's intercession in the matter of ladino hunting in Garza land.

"It is nothing," said Father Mouldoon, "nothing at all compared to what Joel did for me. I only hope that you get along with Don Carlos. He is not the usual *patron* by any means. He is actually kind to his people, and that is why I can be his friend, also."

"You take your work very seriously, Father," Ewen said admiringly. "I have admired you, personally, for a long time."

"Thank you, Captain Cameron," the priest said genially.

"Are you leaving Agua Dulce now, Father?"

"Yes. I have been here several days already."

"Do you come often?"

"Every six months or so. More than my duties require. I am comfortable here, and I let that sway me." The priest lifted his hand. *"Vaya con Dios, amigos."*

"Vaya con Dios, Father," Ewen said courteously.

Finally Canales succeeded in pinning Don Carlos down to serious talk. Ever since 1837, political intrigue had occupied the Spanish-speaking peoples along the Rio Grande. Now they were seeking to combine all the various factions against the Texians. That meant accepting Santa Anna's leadership. There was no other choice, Manuel argued. They could not unseat the dictator; therefore they must join him. The future of Mexico demanded aggressive action against Texas. France and England were unwilling to lend Mexico more money until Santa Anna's government proved itself. At least Mexico must show its willingness to protect her boundaries. European capitals had been shocked by the bold action of Jack Hays and his rangers when they rode to Laredo and raised the Lone Star flag over the plazas of that Mexican town. Mexico must strike back.

"An invasion costs money," Canales told the wealthy *proprietor.* "The treasury is empty. Santa Anna means to organize and equip an army at his own expense, but—"

"With funds he embezzled from the government," Don Carlos interrupted. "The man has no means of his own. He was a nobody until he usurped command of the army."

Canales shrugged that comment aside. He did not wish to discuss military leaders who used their prestige for personal gain. Patriotism was certainly not his own sole motive in the forthcoming campaign.

"He is Mexico's strong man," Manuel said. "Only he can properly organize an army for an invasion. He has chosen a Frenchman to command his forces, General Adrian Woll, who had a brilliant record in Europe. I have watched his troops drill. Such precision! I do not see how any Texian force can stand up against his lancers."

Don Carlos frowned. He personally deplored violence, but he had followed his father's example in maintaining a well-armed vaquero force.

"I'm not certain that regular troops are the answer for Texians," the older man said slowly. "I understand they are learning to be good horsemen. And it would take a thousand of your lancers to wipe out my vaqueros."

"In the brush, yes. But San Antonio de Bexar is not in the *monte*. Woll will have the artillery to shell the town if need be. Our misfortune at San Jacinto was only bad luck, sir. All military experts say that."

"I have read the same thing about Napoleon at

Waterloo," Don Carlos said cryptically. "But no matter. What will this invasion accomplish? How would it better us along the Rio Grande?"

"It will confirm this as Mexican territory. As it is now, you are subject to Texas law."

"Not very," said Garza with a smile. "The only Texians who have come here are *Senor* Cameron's men."

"But you are encouraging them. More will follow after these. Mark my words about that, sir. Give a *Yanqui* an inch and he will seize a mile. Our history proves it. We allowed Stephen F. Austin to settle five hundred families along the Brazos. Ten years later they had seized the entire province for themselves."

"After being provoked into rebellion by this same Santa Anna."

Canales sighed. It was difficult to reason with such a man. "True," he conceded. "Some of our people aided in that rebellion. My uncle to an extent, men like Juan Seguin with their hearts and souls. And look how the Texians rewarded Seguin! By seizing his properties and driving him out of their country—as they call it."

"I hold no brief for Texians," Don Carlos said wearily. "I merely said that they have not bothered me yet." He poured wine for himself and his guest. "We lead a simple life here, Manuel," he said. "Governments do not concern themselves with us, and we do not worry about them. We have always protected ourselves against banditos and Indians, and we shall continue to do that. But intrigue—" he gestured with both hands, "I am too old for that. What help could I contribute, anyhow?"

"Money," Canales said quickly. "His Excellency promises to cancel the back taxes of all *proprietors* who contribute to his campaign. And you must owe a considerable amount in taxes, sir."

"I don't know," Garza said calmly. "I've never paid any."

"None at all?"

"Not one *peso*—to either Mexico or Texas."

The disconcerted Canales could only shake his head. He had expected Don Carlos to be in arrears since the establishment of the Texas Republic, at least. But to have ignored his taxes since 1821, when the new Mexican government had voted assessments on all big landholders!

"And never having been involved with the government," Don Carlos continued, "I will not start now." He refilled their wine glasses. "But I wish you luck with your campaign, my son. What feeling I have is with you."

Manuel realized the futility of further argument. Don Carlos was a stubborn man despite his gentle voice and manners. The captain retired to his room and stretched out for his usual *siesta*. But slumber did not come easily. He had expected great things of this assignment. The wealthy landowners along the Rio Grande could easily afford hand-some contributions to Santa Anna's war chest, a reasonable portion of which Manuel could keep for himself. He had hoped to fill his purse and then win bounty lands for himself because of his military service. He had dreamed of making the leap from soldier to *proprietor* in this single campaign. So far, he mused bitterly, he had accomplished nothing. He could not even claim that Consuela was any closer to accepting him than before.

Joel tethered his pony a safe distance from the hacienda. Circling carefully around the sheds and *jacals*, he reached the larger rear patio unchallenged. Only a few lights still shone in the big house; apparently Don Carlos had retired early. Once Joel heard footsteps coming in his direction and took refuge behind a statue. It proved to be only a *criada*, making sure the outside door was locked, but Joel took no more chances. He was still crouching in his hiding place when Consuela came out of a side door and looked around questioningly.

Softly Joel made a sound like a hoot owl and his eyes danced at her start. Next he cheeped like a bobwhite. This time she located the sound and guessed its origin. A smile curved her lips in spite of her firm intention to show disapproval.

This strapping *Yanqui* was certainly the most uncon-ventional suitor in her experience. Manuel would have already bounded to her side; Ramon would have burst instantly into song. But Joel stepped suddenly out of his hiding place and said, "Hi."

"*Buenos noches*," Consuela said coldly, turning away from him.

But her pretense of pique was wasted. "Sure nice of you to meet me out here, ma'am," he said genially. "Reckon it's a big thing, the way your people look at it."

Consuela did not answer. Actually, she slipped away from Theresa any time she chose. She had met more than one young man on this secluded patio.

"Let's sit down," Joel said, taking her hand before she realized what he was about. She let herself be pulled down beside him on a stone bench beneath the banana clumps. "This brush is tough going. Look." And he held out his hands to show his scratched palms.

Consuela stared. She was not accustomed to young men who so casually, even a bit proudly, showed evidence of physical toil.

"You should have vaqueros."

"Yep, we should," agreed Joel. He shifted around, crossing his long legs. "I've been figgering about that. How does your granddad pay these people?"

51

"What do you mean?" she asked, completely puzzled.

"He hires 'em, doesn't he?"

"Why, no," said the perplexed girl. "Not exactly." She struggled to find words to explain. "They belong to the land," she told him. "They live here and so, of course, they do my grand-father's bidding. Everyone does."

"What's to stop 'em from picking up and leaving?"

"Where could they go?"

"They could catch on with another *proprietor*, couldn't they?"

"Of course not. They belong here."

He considered this a moment, then shook his head. "Never thought of it that way. They're sort of slaves, then?"

"Not at all," Consuela denied quickly. "They're free people. They come and go as they please."

"But you said they couldn't leave."

"They don't *want* to leave. They don't even think about leaving. They belong here."

"Well," said Joel with a sigh, "I see we don't get anywhere with that."

Her eyes twinkled. "You do not understand my country, *Senor* Ho-el."

"I sure don't," he admitted. His eyes swept her face. "But I think I'm gonna like learning about it," he added. "Especially with so pert a teacher."

He had wondered all afternoon just how he

would act if and when he had this lovely creature within arm's reach. He had tried to get some advice from the more experienced Curly, but Wilkins had helped him little. All Curly could tell him was that one of the *rico* could not be wooed like a pueblo *nina*. Aristocratic maidens posed high on their pedestals and their swains knelt humbly at their feet. But Joel had no intention of doing any such thing. He held Consuela O'Rourke in some awe, but still he had not acted as if she were some ethereal creature. He had treated her as he would have any pretty American girl who aroused his admiration, and she seemed to like it. She had slipped out of the house to meet him, hadn't she? She had left that fancy-frocked captain to his own devices while she sat on a bench with a brushpopper who made no bones about his station in life.

"I'm sure gonna like learning—from you," he said.

Consuela, her hands folded in her lap, did not meet his eyes. She was uncertain what to do about Joel's plain intention of putting his arm around her. There came his fingers, gently grasping her shoulder.

"I cannot stay but a moment, *senor*," she said. He filled her with confusion, and she resented it. Always before it had been the other way around. "My grandfather would punish me if he knew I was here. And I don't know what he would do to you."

"Let me worry about that," said Joel, his arm tightening around her. "Reckon he'd have to catch me first."

Consuela decided to ignore his arm. "Do you think you could outrun my grandfather's charros?"

"Afoot or on horseback," Joel said.

"You are not modest, *senor*," Consuela scolded. She pushed up and adopted a reproachful attiude. "In fact, you are entirely too bold. I am not sure I can meet you again."

"You have to," declared Joel, feeling surer of himself now. He had flustered her, and he knew that was a good sign. "We got unfinished business."

"What?"

"You haven't told me everything. I want to learn how to run a rancho."

"See my grandfather," said Consuela with a toss of her head.

"Maybe I will—later." Joel grinned down at her. "Tomorrow night?"

Consuela hesitated, then shook her head. She must spend some time with Manuel. After all, he had crossed the Rio Grande to see her and to ignore him further would arouse suspicion. Joel was no good at concealing his emotions. She smiled at his rueful expression.

"The night after, maybe," Consuela said archly. "We shall see."

Chapter Five

Ewen Cameron watched Joel practice with his five-shooters. He would stride along, whirl suddenly, whip out both weapons and fire at a *huisache* trunk. He improved each day; his bullets sent bark flying.

Ewen nursed a smile. In two years, the Scot mused, Joel had grown into quite a man. A fighter, for sure; such a frontier produced them. But in other ways, too. Cameron heartily approved of Joel's ambition to develop his own rancho. The traffic in wild cattle would not last forever.

Joel sat down by the Scot to clean his smoking pistols.

"That was quite a present Walker gave you," Ewen said. "Samuel Colt could sell a thousand of those guns if he could get them to Texas."

"They're handy things," nodded Joel. "You can turn a ladino with 'em."

Ewen's eyes twinkled. "I want to ask you something. I understand you have been back to the hacienda."

Joel didn't deny it.

"Curly told me there are some Mexican dragoons lurking around," continued Ewen. "Three of them besides Captain Canales."

Joel shook his head. He hadn't noticed any such soldiers.

"They could only be his personal entourage," brooded the Scot. "Canales may be north of the Rio only to court Don Carlos' granddaughter. Do you suppose they are betrothed?"

Joel scowled. They might be at that. It was a sickening thought. Then he shrugged his shoulders. She had not acted as if she were betrothed. Perhaps Canales merely assumed so; or had Don Carlos' commitment.

"Canales may have nothing more than romance on his mind," said Ewen, failing to notice Joel's preoccupation, "but I hesitate to believe it. All of his family are conspirators. I wish I could spare a man to send to San Antonio. Captain Hays should know that Canales is here."

Joel hid his thoughts. As much as he appreciated the Scot, he had learned some of Ewen's weaknesses. Bitterness toward anything and anybody Mexican was certainly one of them. Ewen could act with courtesy and even persuasiveness when it meant a profit, as in his dealings with Don Carlos. But he would never forgive or forget the treachery he had encountered below the Rio Grande.

"But we are too short-handed for that," Ewen decided. "Just keep your eyes open, lad. If we see anything like a company of lancers, I'll ride to tell Hays myself."

That closed the subject. Joel, however, did not forget the conversation. It was hard for him to imagine Canales as a potentially dangerous conspirator. Let the captain conspire against Texas all he wished; it would never amount to anything. But as a rival for Consuela O'Rourke's favors—that was a horse of a different color. Joel could not imagine Consuela actually loving such a person as Canales, but maybe her grandfather would insist upon such a marriage, even without love, and custom would require her dutiful submission. Then another thought worried him. Perhaps this dark-eyed girl was simply amusing herself with him. His jaw set as he stretched out on his bedroll to stare up at the stars. Well, if that was her game, he would find it out the next time she got within reach of his arms.

Consuela sensed Manuel's determination and tried to avoid being alone with him. But finally his opportunity came. He told her in glowing details of the military coup which would make him a rich man. When Mexican mastery of the area between the Nueces and the Rio Grande had been established he would own a *porcion* comparable to her grandfather's. Then, when he had lifted himself to her station, would she marry him?

His carefully rehearsed words left her some- what saddened, but unshaken. At first she tried to parry him.

"That is in the future," she said. "We shall see, Manuel."

He shook his head. This invasion of Texas was no remote dream. Already troops were quietly gathering at Guerrero. General Adrian Woll would cross the Rio Grande in August.

"So soon?" she asked faintly.

"So soon," Manuel affirmed, a triumphant note in his voice. The next Christ's birthday should see him owning his own land.

Consuela sighed. She must answer directly, she saw that. "I do not love you, Manuel," she said gently. "And I have my mother's memory still with me. She married only for love, and she was happy with her Irishman until she died."

She tried to ease his disappointment. "Oh, I know I am stubborn and horrid, Manuel. My grandfather tells me so every time he is put out with me, and that is often enough. Father Muldoon scolds me, too. He tells me I will never grow into a good woman until I have become a good wife. And I am fond of you. I admire your bravery and your devotion to your country. But—"

Her words died off and her eyes fell. Manuel's eyes burned.

"Very well, *querida mia*," he said sadly. He hesitated, then sat beside her on the same stone bench where Joel's arm had draped lightly over her shoulders. "You must tell me this, then. Is there another, Consuela? I must know if there is ever a chance for me."

Consuela bit her lip. What was there to tell him? Was she sure of anything except that this Joel Howard affected her as no other suitor ever had? One instant he amused her, the next she was confused. One moment she wanted to tease him mercilessly, then without reason she was tempted to cradle his shaggy, coppery head on her bosom and murmur soft words in his ear. Nor was that all she felt about this *Yanqui*. She was actually a little afraid of him. He grew a bit bolder each time she saw him. And she was certain that he was a man who would not step back.

"I don't know, Manuel," she said. "I just don't know."

Manuel's dark eyes flashed. The American. Who else? The towering *Yanqui* who grinned like a sheep but fought like a panther. Consuela was infatuated with this foreigner, repeating her mother's indiscretion. But history would not repeat itself at Agua Dulce, not completely. Manuel silently swore so as he led Consuela back into the *sala*. This time the clandestine romance would not lead to marriage. There were ways to see that it did not, and Manuel meant to take them.

He disguised his feelings well. Consuela retired to her room convinced that Captain

Canales had accepted his rejection most graciously. She did not know that later that night Canales gathered his retinue of soldiers and gave them curt orders. They were to discard their glittering uniforms so they could move about the rancho without attracting so much attention. They were to keep a close watch on the hacienda day and night. Somehow and some way the *Yanqui* must be meeting Consuela to pay her his strange, uncouth court. And it must be stopped.

Joel washed in the creek and shaved, but did not change to his somber broadcloth suit. Let her see him in homespun shirt and leather leggings. Let her smell the stench of smoke from a hundred campfires, the grease of butchered deer and javelina. Let her compare him to smirking fops like Canales and make her choice. Let it be a quick choice, too, for Joel could not moon forever over a minx who might be laughing at him behind his back. There were more ladinos in this monte than even Ewen Cameron had thought. In a fort-night they would have all the cattle they could drive to Goliad, and then Joel Howard would keep his appointment with Sam Walker and the rangers. They would make this brasada into Texas country, and Joel would come back to it again and again until his spread on the Medina River rivaled these Spanish ranchos in profit if not in area. Grandees like Don Carlos could learn much about turning natural wealth into actual dollars. The idea of scoffing at traffic in wild cattle!

In spite of his mood he was wary about approaching the patio. He crept into the same hiding place behind the statue and waited for Consuela to appear. He had a long time to wait, for in the *sala* Captain Canales sensed Consuela's eagerness to be rid of him and made excuses to keep her downstairs. It was after ten o'clock when she finally managed to slip out the side entrance and into Joel's arms.

For he lost not a second in catching her in close embrace.

"*Senor* Ho-el!" she protested, struggling to get free. But there was no disentangling his strong arms.

His lips clamped down on hers and it was no light, tender kiss. His mouth clung, until desperately she beat his bare head with her small fists.

"Ho-el," she whimpered. "You cannot treat me so. You must not."

"I can't help it," he said, freeing her. "You do that to a man. And I have a notion you do it on purpose."

Consuela gingerly felt her bruised lips. "What do you mean by that?" she demanded.

He tried to hide the triumphant gleam in his

eyes. She had responded to his kiss, and there was no use trying to deny it.

"You wanted me to kiss you," he said lightly. "I just obliged."

"*Senor* Howard, you are impossible!"

But even while her body trembled with anger, she did not turn to leave.

"Oh, I reckon not," said Joel, sinking to the bench and pulling her down beside him. "I reckon I've got you down pat. You're not used to my way of doing things. You're used to leading hombres around the mulberry bush."

"Mulberry bush?"

"Giving 'em the go-around," Joel explained.

Her eyes blazed. "*Senor* Howard, you have said enough!" She stamped her foot and her voice rose. "I have broken the conventions of my people to meet your *Yanqui* customs halfway. I have tolerated your disrespect because I considered that you were expressing yourself in your natural way. But you do not grab me again, *senor.* Understand?"

He said nothing.

"In my country," she snapped, "you ask for a caress. You do not take it by force."

Joel sank down on the stone bench. "Oh, what's the use?" he said despairingly. "You don't understand me." He gestured helplessly. "How can I talk to you?" he asked miserably. "I'm no good at palaver. I took one look at you and I haven't been in my right mind since. You've put all kinds of fool notions in my head."

"Yes, *senor*," she said coldly, "I have."

"And what's wrong with that?" he demanded. "Are you insulted because I'm loco about you? Is it a crime to want to kiss you? Golly moses, *senorita*, I'm human. I can't help it because you can't understand."

"Understand what, *senor*?" she asked softly.

"That I'm crazy about you. That I wish to the dickens I could marry you." Consuela's lips trembled. "Now, either get on back in the house," Joel said desperately, "or sit down here with me and let's talk about it."

Consuela had settled beside him on the bench before she was sure of what she was doing. With the fragrance of her hair in his nostrils, with her hand in his, Joel found it easy to talk. Consuela listened and his words became a confused babble.

For this strange man meant to take her away from Agua Dulce to a new place and a new life. She was afraid to go but she knew that she would, if he were really determined to take her. Every memory was a load weighing her down, keeping her from lifting her tearful face to meet his eagerness. She saw herself as a little girl romping through the cool rooms of the huge adobe house, pestering women at work in the kitchen, stealing sugar from the great dark storeroom, heavy with the smell of chile, onions and coffee. She went again all in white to be received into the arms of the Church. The solemn chanting voices in the background warned her to draw away from this American, but those voices were far away, his right in her ear.

The music out of the past disturbed her, too. She was going to her first *baille* in her first grown-up dress. For the first time, she tingled to her toes as she felt the eyes and hands of men upon her. After that, so many dances, and how she had loved them all! How she had scorned suitors who had cut poor figures at *bailles*!

And Joel Howard promised none of these things. In fact, what he said cast a doubt upon her ever knowing them again. How could she know what to do? How could she tell him in her turn what she felt?

It took a long time, hours. One question tormented them both. How could it be done?

She asked that question and Joel could not answer. Her grandfather would never allow her to wed a man not of their faith. Don Carlos had relented and recognized Terence O'Rourke as a son-in-law, but O'Rourke had fitted himself into their way of life. O'Rourke had become Spanish in everything but name. Joel Howard would not do so. Joel was part and parcel of a puzzling, forbidding breed. His kind meant to rearrange the pattern her people had stamped upon this land. Even a maid dizzy with love could see that.

Nor did Joel deny it. He denied only that the odds were insurmountable. No odds were. If she was willing, he would find a way.

Tears trickled down her cheeks. How could she tell him that she was wiser about such things than he? What could she do but pretend belief in his promises and make the most of the little time they had?

Chapter Six

Corporal Julian Vega dutifully reported to his captain what he had witnessed. *Senorita* Consuela had met the *Yanqui* on the back patio. They had sat in close embrace for a long time. The corporal had not ventured close enough to overhear any of their talk, but obviously the *senorita* and the *Yanqui* were *enamorado*.

Canales chewed on the tips of his mustache. This was not unexpected; he had felt a premonition about this Joel Howard from the beginning. Canales had not considered it a trivial thing when Consuela granted the American's request to dance. *Yanquis*—Manuel hated and feared them.

Canales gave Julian careful orders. The corporal and his two followers were to dog the *Yanqui*'s trail through the *monte*. When the chance came, they were to kill. Then they were to hurry back to the village of Romero, close to the Rio Grande. In no event were they to be seen around Agua Dulce afterward. Don Carlos would not soon forgive a killing on his rancho, not when he had given his personal permission for the Texians to hunt the creek. Don Carlos did not realize that the only way to handle Texians was to shoot them down like dogs. After leaving Agua Dulce, Canales had no further use for his retinue anyhow. His next assignment was to solicit money from the loyal merchants of San Antonio and to confirm their reports about that town's lack of fortifications. Santa Anna was considerably dubious of assurances that San Antonio could be captured with little trouble. He had thought so in 1836, only to lose over a thousand regulars at the Alamo. Canales must enter San Antonio in civilian dress, and without clumsy soldiers at his heels.

Julian was pleased with his orders, especially when the captain promised the three of them a hundred *pesos* each when he rejoined them in Romero. Killing a gringo in the brush—that should be easy. And it would be something to boast about back in Romero. Julian rode off with a wide grin on his pock-marked face.

Joel Howard was plainly worried about something. Curly Wilkins noticed it at breakfast, but kept his peace until they had ridden away from camp.

"What's eating you, son?" he asked then.

"Nothing you can do anything about," Joel said.

Curly suppressed a smile. He guessed his partner's trouble. Cameron's whole crew knew that Joel had been going to the hacienda in the evenings. They thought it a great joke that he had found a *nina*. Only Curly knew that he was meeting Don Carlos' granddaughter, and Wilkins kept that to himself. Joel got enough hoo-rahing as it was. The teasing would be unbearable if the other brushpoppers knew that Joel was mooning around hoping for a *rico* to notice him. Curly was certain that that was the situation, and he pitied his tall partner. The next time, Curly thought, Joel would know better.

The two separated a few miles from camp. The ladinos grew warier every day; no longer could a half-dozen be flushed out of the brush in a matter of minutes. But Joel could not give hunting his full attention, not with the recollection of Consuela's faltering promise weighing on his mind. Last night he had been sure they could sweep aside all obstacles—how could he have believed anything else in his near-delirious state? But this hot, dreary daylight had brought despair. Who could imagine Don Carlos giving up his granddaughter to an itinerant brush-popper? What was to prevent the Spaniard from ordering his vaqueros to rid the *monte* of this troublesome *Yanqui*? No doubt they would relish the assign-ment, too, especially the fearless old man with the short-handled whip. Joel could imagine himself flayed to ribbons and sent on his way.

But he did not intend to give up. That night he would go again to the secluded patio. He would go every night as long as Consuela would meet him. A dreamy expression spread over his features as he rode deeper into the brush. What a fascinating little creature she was! Demure, haughty, pensive, tantalizing—every word he knew described her.

Ahead of him Corporal Julian Vega and his two followers set their ambush. They wore vaquero garb as their captain had ordered, but had kept their lances. These were poised as they waited for the *Yanqui* to ride closer. *"Ahora,"* yelled Julian as Joel reined up his pony to look around for signs of ladinos. Julian burst out of his cover with the two disguised lancers at his heels. Their headlong charge at the gringo did credit to their captain's drilling.

But Joel's wiry chestnut stallion leaped even before its rider saw his danger. And Joel, though almost unseated by his mount's wild lunge, was tugging at his five-shooter even as he fell away from the lance thrusts. Julian's spear raked the chestnut's side; with a wild scream the animal reared high, flailing out at Julian's horse with front hoofs. Holding the chestnut's mane for dear life, Joel held his fire until his mount's four hoofs touched ground again, then shot Julian in the chest. His other two assailants wanted to close in, but their horses balked at colliding with the chestnut. One lancer threw his spear and its point grazed Joel's shoulder. A second quick shot disposed of this adversary and Joel turned to the third. This soldier brought up his single-shot pistol and tried to take careful aim, lying low on his horse's neck to screen himself from Joel's fire. Joel shot into the charger's teeth and the animal leaped sideways. Its rider was an easy target for a foe who still had shots to spare. The lancer toppled from his high-horned saddle and Joel sat his calmed mustang looking down at three dead men.

Slipping to the ground, he studied the bodies one after the other. Except for Julian Vega's pock-marked features he saw nothing unusual. Brown-skinned men, Indians or Mexicans, whatever they should be called. Vaqueros, too; Don Carlos' natives. Joel took out his soiled kerchief and wiped his sweaty face. Now that it was all over he was trembling. And he felt slightly nauseated. He had shot instinctively, in self-defense. Except for the gun given him by Sam Walker he would have been helpless against three assailants.

Curly Wilkins came tearing through the brush to see what the shooting was about.

"I'll be gol-darned!" Curly gasped when he saw the three lifeless bodies. He stirred Vega's head and shoulders with the toe of his boot. "Ugly coot, ain't he?"

"Plenty ugly," Joel muttered. "Looked meaner with a spear in his hand than he does now."

"Don Carlos' vaqueros?" Curly asked.

"I reckon."

"I knew you were letting yourself in for it,"

said Curly with a sigh. "So did Ewen. But we couldn't tell you. You wouldn't listen."

A cold smile came to Joel's lips. "And I'm not listening now," he snapped. "I'm taking Consuela whether Don Carlos likes it or not."

Curly shook his head. "You loco fool. You got three of 'em quicker than a cat can lick his whiskers. You caught 'em with their britches down. They didn't sabbe a five-shooter. But there's a hundred more of 'em. Next time the Don will send a pack."

"He'd better hurry, then," shrugged Joel. "I'm lighting out with her tonight."

Curly stared at his tall friend. "You're wolfing, ain't you?"

"Wait and see."

Curly whistled. "Where'll you head?"

"My cabin."

Curly took a deep breath. "You got a horse for her to ride?"

"No," Joel said. He hadn't thought of that.

"Long way to ride double," said Curly. "Waldo has a gentle pony. I'll trade him out of it."

Joel nodded. He appreciated his friend's help.

"You'll need more blankets and grub," mused Curly. "And I'll tag along tonight to cover for you."

Consuela came quietly out the door and slipped into Joel's arms without saying a word. He kissed

71

her quickly and held her at arm's length to see what kind of dress she wore. Blouse and skirt, thin, sheer blouse. Should he send her back for other garments? He decided against it.

Joel lifted Consuela in his arms.

"What are you doing, Joel?" she demanded. But she did not struggle.

He bent down and kissed her. "Ask me no questions and I'll tell you no lies," he said.

She buried her face against his. Her thought was that he was carrying her into the shadows, safely away from the house, and with a shiver she anticipated what would happen there. She had known ever since last night that this tall *Yanqui* would not be satisfied with kisses and caresses. She knew what he meant to do and she knew she would not try to stop him. Not until they reached the horses did she suspect anything else. Then another man appeared out of nowhere to ask if all was set. Joel swung up on his horse with her still in his arms.

"No, Joel!" Consuela cried out suddenly, struggling to break free. "Mother of God, no!"

But it was too late. The stallion beneath her broke into a swinging lope. The arms encircling her were like bands of steel. And Joel Howard rode on, impervious to both her protestations and her tears.

Chapter Seven

Mutely Consuela let herself be set onto Waldo Prewitt's saddle. She clung to its high horn for support as the mare followed Joel's chestnut. She had sobbed herself into exhaustion. Throbbing aches beat against her forehead like heavy hammers. All this seemed unreal to her. Snatched up, held in the saddle for miles, then placed on another horse and led still farther on! It was maddening. She hated Joel for doing this to her, yet she gloried in his daring, his forcefulness. He could have managed it no other way.

It was all she could do to stay in the saddle. Beast of a man—he had not stopped to think that she had never ridden astride before in her life! Didn't he know that when highborn *senoritas* rode at all, it was on a small gentle mule and side-saddle? And such riding as he was compelling her to do! Mile after mile, hour after hour. Where was he taking her, to the end of the earth? Daylight came and he still kept going. The sun rose high, searing her neck and shoulders. She knew she was reddening.

Finally Joel pulled to a stop, but not out of pity for her; only to water his horse and hers, then take up their killing pace anew. Her eyes ached; heavy weights pressed down on their lids. By now the torture to her body had eased; she was numbed to pain. On and on, the chestnut swinging along with an occasional snort, the mare clomping behind. The thought came to her dulled mind that her grandfather's vaqueros would never pursue them so far.

In a daze she realized the horses were slowing down. An instant later she was lifted out of the saddle and placed tenderly on a blanket. She fell sound asleep at once.

She awoke to find Joel close by, squatting Indian-fashion.

"Thought you were going to sleep all day," he said cheerfully. "We just stopped for a *siesta*, not for the night."

Consuela struggled up to a sitting position.

"We gotta push on," he said, rising. "Next water is the Frio and that's a right smart ride."

Consuela realized for the first time that they had stopped by a sluggish stream.

"What river is this?" she asked faintly.

"Nueces."

She brushed back several rebellious strands of hair. "How far have we come already?"

"A good piece." A grin broke across his face. "Far enough to shake your grandfather's vaqueros." He held out his hand. "But we're still a long way from home. Let's get moving."

Consuela tried, then sank back. "I can't," she whimpered. And she couldn't. The muscles in her legs and thighs were too stiff for movement. She groaned with another futile effort, then forced a weak smile. "I'm too sore to walk. You'll have to lift me."

Joel picked her up without another word. She was a dead weight in his arms; he watched her a moment after setting her in the saddle. But she took the reins with one limp hand and caught the horn with her other and he decided she could manage. He swung up on the chestnut. The mustang was sluggish but Joel waited a while before using his spurs. Occasionally he looked back to see how Consuela was doing. He had worn her to a nub, he thought ruefully. But what else could he have done? A slower pace might have cost him his ears.

Consuela was nodding in the saddle as if half asleep. Joel watched her a moment approvingly. Maybe she had never ridden much before, but she was getting the hang of it, giving and rising with the mare's gait. There was a trick to it; a man had to learn. And anything a man had learned about horsemanship before mounting a mustang had to be learned over again. Ewen Cameron claimed a man who had become expert with hunters or trotters made a poor cowboy. Cowboy —how Ewen hated that description of himself.

Joel looked back at Consuela again. She was sitting up straighter, looking around her as if curious about this different terrain. It was

75

changing, all right. They were coming out of the *brasada* and into the post oak belt. The Medina River wasn't too far away.

But they had a stop to make before going on to Joel's cabin. Helena was no real town, only a few shelters grouped behind Preacher Scott's combination saloon and general store. Joel tenderly lifted Consuela out of the saddle.

"What is this?" she asked, unimpressed with either Preacher or his establishment.

"We got a paper to sign," Joel said. Scott nodded as Joel explained. Preacher served a wide stretch of country as notary public. He had prepared such testimonials before. Joel Howard and Consuela O'Rourke pledged themselves to marry properly when the chance came. That made them man and wife under Texas laws. Such concessions were necessary in so unsettled a land.

Consuela wrote her name without hesitation, then they were riding again. They were almost there, Joel assured her.

Consuela slid off the mare into Joel's arms. He held her close for a moment, then allowed her to stand. He pointed to the cabin.

"There she is," he said. "Such as she is."

A frown creased Consuela's sun-burned forehead as she looked around her in wonder. She saw the boxlike structure of logs with

76

deerhide flaps over its openings, a heap of drying logs, a brush lean-to, a shallow spring seeping out of the hillside, a pole corral. Beyond this small clearing flowed the Medina River; Joel's cabin stood in the fringe of its timbered bottom.

Consuela brushed hair out of her eyes. Her lips trembled as her eyes came back to Joel's.

"Is this all of it?" she asked faintly.

His gleam slowly died. "So far. All I've had time to do."

She shook her dark head. Live here—how could she? Even the *jacals* behind her grandfather's hacienda had more comforts than she saw here.

"Can we live somewhere else—until it's finished?"

Hers was a weak inquiry, a well-meaning one. Her tears had dried long since. Except for her aches and her overwhelming fatigue she was in high spirits. The farther they rode away from Agua Dulce the better she felt about what they had done. Or what Joel had done.

Joel shook his head. "There's nowhere else. I reckon our nearest neighbor is twenty miles off." He took her arm. "I'll show you the inside."

She let herself be led to the biggest opening. Joel threw back the rawhide flap. The interior was bare except for a hand-hewn table, a bench and shelves. He had tamped the dirt floor but hadn't covered its bareness. Next Consuela noticed the wide bunk: rawhide stretched tight

77

across stout timbers. The fireplace opening was wide and deep; it drew perfectly, Joel told her proudly. He had been doubtful of his ability to build a fireplace that wouldn't smoke.

Consuela sat down on the crude bench. Joel studied her and his mouth tightened.

"It isn't much, is it?"

Tears welled in her eyes. "I don't see how we can live here. I just don't."

"Couples have started out on less," he said coldly. "A lot less. I tried to tell you. I reckon you just couldn't believe me—how little there is like you're used to."

A roach scrambled across the packed dirt; Joel crushed it underfoot. "There's water, wood and meat," he said tonelessly. "There's salt and some corn meal. We won't starve and we won't freeze in a norther. I'll start on a roof the first thing in the morning. I'll lay a floor next. We'll be fixed up real cozy by winter, see if we aren't."

Consuela nodded but refused to look up. Joel stared down at her a moment, then walked to the horses. He took off saddles and bridles and hung them carefully on pegs in the brush lean-to. He prodded the weary animals into the pole corral and fastened its makeshift gate. Then, rifle in the crotch of his arm, he told Consuela he was going after a deer.

"Reckon you're hungry," he said gruffly. "I danged sure am. I'll be back pronto."

She bobbed her head in response. Joel turned on his heel and strode downstream. Not over a mile from his cabin was a salt lick; never before had he failed to sight deer there in late afternoon. He walked swiftly, raging to himself. What had she expected? Hadn't he done his best to prepare her for his half-finished cabin and its wild surroundings? Hadn't he told her about purposely locating well away from the settlements, beating other land-hungry men to a choice river bottom? Hadn't he courted her in buckskin shirt and homespun breeches so she'd know exactly what kind of man he was and how he lived?

He wasn't so preoccupied that he didn't sight the doe and fawn bolting away from his approach. He took quick aim at the smaller animal and it dropped, stone dead. Joel gutted it on the spot and swung the carcass over his shoulder. This was no great shucks of a kill but it was meat. He was near-starved himself and he was sure Consuela was hungry, too. Poor thing, she wasn't used to hardships.

Maybe she never would be. He brooded about that as he trudged back with his kill. She had every right to be miserable with what she had found on the Medina. No way to make it easier for her.

Consuela was still inside the cabin. Joel turned his back to the door and started butchering the fawn. He hung the carcass from a convenient limb and first carefully pulled off the hide. Then he sliced away the ribs and cracked the animal's backbone. Looking up suddenly, his eyes met hers. Consuela had come noiselessly closer. She was watching him, fascinated by his quick, sure motions. Joel did not know it, but she was very impressed. One minute there had been nothing in sight to eat; the next instant he was preparing meat to cook, and doing it expertly. Such a man, she was thinking, could manage his own existence wherever he was. And his mate's, too.

"We'll eat," Joel said gruffly.

Consuela nodded. She was certainly hungry. She watched him wide-eyed. He started a fire with leaves, twigs and two rough-edged stones. He whittled oak branches into spits. Squatting on his haunches, he broiled chunks of meat over the flames. All this time he was silent, almost indifferent to her presence, and Consuela whimpered to herself. There was no use of his treating her so coldly. Could she help her disappointments and apprehensions?

"Here," he said, handing her one of the spits. "This'll cure what ails you."

It satisfied her hunger, all right. She nibbled, at first; she had never eaten without knives and forks before. But the meat tasted good and she was famished. Shortly she was ripping the flesh with her teeth and bolting down her bites. Joel grunted and held ribs over the blaze. "Nothing wrong with your appetite," he said.

Consuela didn't bother to answer; she just kept eating. Finally both of them had enough. Joel stomped out the small fire and wiped his greasy mouth. Then he looked down at her as if she were a stranger, not the young woman he had stolen from her grandfather's hacienda.

"No call for you to take on any more," he said. "We'll start back at daylight."

Consuela stared at him. "Start back?" she asked faintly. Was there no end to the surprises about this tall rawboned man?

"Sure," he said gruffly. He leaned against a tree trunk, picking his teeth with a twig. "Reckon I was plumb crazy to let it go this far. I can't help that now. But I'll get you back to your grandfather."

"Joel," she protested, tearful again. "I don't understand."

"It's plain to me," he shrugged. "I reckon you took a shine to me, all right. But you're sick of the deal and I don't blame you a danged bit."

Consuela stared at the ground. What a man— could he do nothing right! Ride her almost to her death and then decide to take her back.

"I am not going," she snapped.

His eyes went wide. "You won't—go back!"

She leaped to her feet. She had to laugh then, in spite of her anger. Poor simple dolt!

"Joel," she said scornfully, "you are the biggest fool of a man to ever live."

His expression slowly changed. A grin formed on his bony features. "I know it," he sighed. "I don't know the first thing about women." He took a deep breath. "But I can see that I'm going to learn in a hurry."

The days flew. Joel realized that they had lived together on the Medina for a full week. And, he reflected ruefully, he had done precious little about getting the cabin ready for winter.

It was high time to be up and doing. The garments Consuela had worn from Agua Dulce were dirty and in rags. The cabin needed a thorough cleaning. Let her do that while he rode to Helena for supplies.

Helena—she recalled the place after a moment. That was where they had signed the document which legalized their union in Texas.

How far away was it? If he rode hard, he answered, he could go and come in a single day and night. Consuela's tears flowed at once. He mustn't leave her alone for that long. She was helpless in that wild spot without him.

Joel shook his head. She had to learn how to care for herself. And how to do the work of a household, too. From now on he'd be too busy to wait on her hand and foot.

"Did I ask to be brought here?" she demanded heatedly. "Tell me that."

He had temper, too. "You danged sure didn't have to stay," he shot back. "I offered to take you right back."

Consuela could vent her anger in Spanish better than in English, so Joel understood only snatches of her tirade. If he wanted a *peon*, why hadn't he grabbed one of the *ninas* around the pueblo? Most of them worshipped gringos and would be glad to double as his household slave and *querida*. She was highborn herself, as he'd known full well. She was used to servants and turning to a well-filled pantry for her wants. Why should he expect her to learn overnight how to shift for herself in an empty wilderness? Maybe she'd never learn. Maybe he'd be forced to get a *criedo* to do the chores and she wasn't worth that much trouble.

He couldn't match her angry outburst, couldn't begin to. Consuela could scream three words to his one and in two languages. Finally Joel just saddled his chestnut and rode off. All he could do, he mused miserably, was to hope she had worked herself out of that state by the time he returned.

Preacher Scott had few customers, but these usually bought heavily, and he made money. His

83

was the last store a brushpopping crew passed going after ladinos and the first stop when driving a herd back to market. He sold baled wild hay and grain as well as staple groceries, powder, lead and whiskey.

He greeted Joel sourly, not because of any dislike, but because that was his normal treatment of customers. Preacher wasted no amenities on his grizzled clientele. They wanted his merchandise and he wanted their cash money— no Republic of Texas currency accepted. The only personal service he rendered was to pass on oral and written messages.

Joel asked for information about the comings and goings of cowboy crews. Preacher nodded. He did know something of interest.

"Ewen got chased away from his trap," he said tersely. "That Don something-or-other jumped him out with a whole army. Made 'em pack up and git. Couldn't even drive out what they had caught. Ewen's been cursing you ever since. Swears you'll never go out with him again."

Joel sighed. He wasn't surprised.

"Did they have a fight?"

"Nope. The greasers took 'em flat-footed. Curly Wilkins—he went for his rifle. The greaser *caporal* near cut off his hand with a whip."

Joel nodded, remembering the expert way the white-mustached vaquero had handled his whip.

Joel carefully selected items from Preacher's wide variety of stock. He bought flour, dried beans and fruit, salt, sugar, pepper, seed corn, blankets, powder and lead, needles, thread and a half-bolt of calico cloth. He had such a pile that Preacher sold him two treated hides to make his bundles.

The chestnut was so heavily loaded that Joel allowed it to walk. Darkness caught him halfway home. He spread one of the new blankets and tried not to think about Consuela. He could imagine how she was suffering this night. But that couldn't be helped. They needed everything he had bought. He couldn't lighten the duties she would have to take over, either. She must learn to cook and make her own clothes and help him with chores like dropping corn and curing hides. And if she didn't have the spunk to face it, they might as well settle things now.

Then he groaned in his sleep and reached to caress a soft figure that wasn't there. He came wide awake in disappointment at not finding her convenient to his touch. Dang it, she had him in the palm of her hand.

Chapter Eight

He reined up at the edge of the clearing. What if Consuela greeted him with more temper and more tearful reproaches? Could he treat her firmly?

He grunted and rode on. He might as well get the reception over with, whatever it would be. He swung down from the chestnut and started unfastening his bundles.

"Joel—Joel!"

He turned to face her. She flung her arms around his neck and clung tightly.

"You were gone so long," she whispered in his ear.

But she wasn't nagging. She pulled away and proudly showed what she had done in his absence. She had cleaned the cabin without any sort of a broom. She had scrubbed his spare shirt and breeches. She had washed their blankets, too, falling into the river and getting herself soaked. Oh, she was a sight trying to do things for herself! She was happy that he hadn't been there to laugh at her. She had meant to cook meat but couldn't start a fire. What in the world was Joel going to do with her!

He answered with a bear hug. The weight of the world had dropped off his shoulders.

"Don't you worry," he assured her. "You'll catch on. You gotta try, though. And throwing a temper fit like you did yesterday—"

"I was awful," she softly agreed. "God told me I was."

"What?"

"Of course. Oh, I was furious with you, Joel. I was going to start home afoot."

"You what? Why, you'd have been lost before—"

"No, I wouldn't," she interrupted simply. "Not if God had wanted me to go. I prayed to Him first. I never thought of starting out without doing that. You were just gone when I started to make my own crucifix. I took two of those poles and tied them with vines and picked out a pretty spot by the river and—"

She stopped short. Joel was staring at her and she couldn't understand his expression.

"Why, what's the matter?"

Joel shook his head. "Nothing."

"I wanted some kind of a chapel," Consuela continued. "I took your axe and cut some limbs and tried to use vines to hold them up but everything kept falling down. Finally I just stuck the crucifix in the ground and prayed anyhow. And I learned I was acting like a spoiled, selfish child. I was trying to have my happiness without paying for it. I wanted to be your wife without doing your wife's work. So I confessed my selfishness and laziness and prayed to God for the strength to bear my share of our load. Then I got up and came back and started trying to do things. I haven't done much and I've done that poorly, but I have tried, Joel. And I'm going to try harder."

Joel didn't know what to say. He'd never dealt with such a guileless, honest admission. Consuela's clear, shining eyes confirmed her sincerity and determination.

"You need a strong, busy woman," she added. "I'm not sure I'll ever be strong enough, but I'll be busy. You must teach me, Joel. I know so little."

"You'll do," Joel said huskily, pulling her to him. "Just don't you worry about a thing. We're going to do all right."

This miraculous change in her attitude was something for Joel to think about as he looked for his scattered cattle. He found her crude crucifix and the tree trimmings she couldn't manage. It was exactly as she described, two short poles bound into a cross. Joel didn't trust himself to ask questions about her experiences with prayer. There was no doubting her story; her cheerful manner bore it out. She woke as early as he and insisted on her own awkward effort before allowing him to start the fire. She'd learn to do it yet, she vowed.

She showed quick sabbe about some things, a near helpless approach to others. She quickly learned to broil meat and to mix sourdough bread. She called upon imagination and faint recollections for ways to season meat, beans and dried fruit. Joel knew half-forgotten tricks himself; with only his own appetite to satisfy, he had cooked what was the least trouble. His grandmother, he remembered, had considered wild dandelions edible. One of Ewen's negro cooks had occasionally varied their fare with stewed squirrel and sourdough dumplings. Joel knew at least the rudiments of making soap; he killed two javelinas and stripped off layers of fat to boil and congeal. It was strong soap but it certainly cleaned everything it touched.

He herded his cattle back to the valley, then let the animals roam again. They'd drift shorter distances each time; cows bunched close with only two bulls to lead them off. Joel counted sixty-two calves. Forty were bull yearlings that he could market without slowing the growth of his herd. His gross should be six hundred dollars, at least; yearlings might bring a higher price than an unculled bunch of ladinos.

He worked his cattle in the mornings— castrating the yearlings, branding and dehorning. Afternoons he worked on the cabin, splitting slab shingles for the roof. Between times he slipped away from Consuela to labor on a surprise for her. Since these daily prayers meant so much, she should have a decent chapel. Nothing fancy, but a shelter where she could kneel before a more impressive crucifix. He shaped the cross out of cedar, polished it to a gleaming surface. The chapel was a tiny building when finished, only large enough for one person at a time. But Consuela was delighted and Joel beamed at her appreciation.

"It's good for you," he said lightly. "Let you miss a day at your prayers and you're not worth shooting."

She giggled. That was Father Muldoon's doing, she explained. He was tolerant of some sins, but adamant about daily worship.

"You should have known him better, Joel. There's no kinder, wiser man anywhere."

Joel could believe that. No lesser man could have won Ewen Cameron's whole-hearted respect.

Time flew by for Joel. His only complaint was the days were too short. The month of August was almost gone and it seemed to him very little was done.

Consuela still claimed his attention. She wanted a doeskin skirt and he tried to teach her how to cure hides. He ended up by doing it himself, and then cutting the skins to pattern. With her only frock torn and frayed, she needed garments in a hurry. Nothing but a loose-fitting blouse resulted from her efforts with the cloth he had brought from Helena.

But she stayed cheerful and willing; and could

kiss and tease away his impatiences. Someday, sometime, the roof would get finished and the floor laid and enough meat cured to feed them. And Consuela's happiness matched his except for one gnawing worry. Her daily visits to her private chapel only aggravated that concern. Finally she demanded that Joel do something about it.

They weren't married in the eyes of her Church, she pointed out. She couldn't expect full forgiveness until that was rectified. And she didn't believe Father Muldoon would condone their post-poning banns any longer.

Sure he would, argued Joel. The Brazos settlements were full of couples whose tardy rites had been solemnized by the Irish priest.

Consuela shook her head. That wasn't for her. She wanted to return to Agua Dulce and get her grandfather's forgiveness. Father Muldoon would come up from Guerrero or Mier to marry them even if he had to make a special trip. She was sure he would.

"And we'd better go right away," she insisted.

Joel hemmed.

"What about San Antonio? Won't we find a priest there?"

Consuela refused to consider that, either. She wanted her grandfather's forgiveness. Her penance wouldn't be complete until Don Carlos had recognized her marriage, too. And she was sure she could appease her grandparent. He had never been able to deny her anything.

Joel's eyes hardened. Her grandfather's vaqueros, he said grimly, weren't about to get another chance at him.

"What do you mean?"

He told her tersely about the attempt to kill him. "They thought I was plumb easy," he finished. "They didn't know about five-shooters."

Consuela looked at him wide-eyed. She couldn't imagine her kindly grandfather ordering three of his vaqueros to ambush anyone.

"He danged sure did," said Joel with a shrug. "They jumped me not five miles from Ewen's camp. Rose up right out of the brush and came at me with lances."

"Lances?"

"Sure, spears."

"Joel," she protested, "our vaqueros never carry lances. They have muskets—Grandfather bought a hundred rifles not too long ago. And he buys powder and lead. But the vaqueros don't use lances. Whips, yes."

"I was there," he said ruefully. "I was the hombre they tried to get. I reckon I know."

"I don't understand it," Consuela frowned. "I'm almost positive that Grandfather didn't even know I was meeting you. He never catches on to such things—and I can't believe any *criedo* told him. Or my *duenna*, either." Consuela thought about it. "And Grandfather would have given his orders to Juan, not anybody else. Juan's awfully touchy about that. Most *caporals* are. The *patron* tells the *caporal* what he wants done and that's all."

Joel shook his head. "Juan wasn't in the bunch. Not if he's the old geezer with the short-handled whip."

"He is. He's seventy if he's a day but he's still the best *caporal* anywhere. And a whip is the only weapon he'll carry."

"He had nothing to do with it," Joel repeated. "It happened so quick I wasn't sure, but that pock-marked hombre seemed to be giving the orders. The other two came right at his heels."

"Pock-marked?"

"All over his face. About as ugly a character as I ever saw."

"Pock-marked," Consuela said slowly. "And there were three of them?" Her dark eyes suddenly flashed. "Joel, those weren't our vaqueros at all. Those were the three soldiers Manuel Canales brought to Agua Dulce."

She continued as Joel looked doubtful. "Of course they were," she cried. "I can see it all now. Manuel was put out with me because I wouldn't give him any encouragement. He didn't say much but I could tell he was upset. Manuel asked me if there was anybody else and I tried to evade answering. So he spied on me and found out about us and decided to get rid of you, and set his soldiers to do it."

The more Joel thought about her version, the easier it was to believe. Manuel Canales had impressed him as a man who'd send others to do his killing.

"Oh, he came to Agua Dulce with such a big dream," continued Consuela. "He's poor, you know, no estate of any kind. He has high connections but no property. And he's always been involved in political intrigue. He hates Texians and he's eager to fight for Mexico. This invasion has presented him a great opportunity. If he gets the help of the *proprietors* along the Rio Grande—"

Joel rose up. "What invasion?" he demanded.

"The one they're planning," Consuela said a little impatiently. "Manuel is one of the ring-leaders."

"You mean he's plotting an invasion of Texas?"

"Of course," she said innocently. "He usually is. That's why he was at Agua Dulce—to ask my grandfather for money. They have their army already organized. They don't need volunteers, just money. And if the plot is successful, Manuel expects to get a *porcion* as his reward. And maybe a high governmental position, too, when the State of Taumalipas is reorganized. There isn't much to it as it is, not with Texas claiming everything between the Nueces and the Rio Grande."

Joel caught her shoulders. Who cared what Manuel Canales hoped to gain for himself! What about this army already organized for invasion?

She told him all she knew, and she knew enough to shock him. The Mexican forces were gathering at Guerrero. They would cross the Rio Grande in boats and march upon San Antonio by the half-forgotten *camino real* leading through the *monte.* That way they'd avoid contact with Jack Hays' rangers on the road between Bexar and Laredo.

When was this march supposed to start? Consuela couldn't be sure, except that Manuel had hinted it would be soon. Judging from what he had said she would guess around the first of September.

The first of September! It was the first time Consuela had ever heard Joel blaze out. She didn't like it. Nor did she like the sudden change in his manner. He acted as if she had some responsibility for this scheme. She misinterpreted his feeling, of course. What disgusted him was the precious time lost because he hadn't known of this plot sooner. Ewen Cameron had suspected that Canales was at Agua Dulce for no good purpose. Ewen had commented that Jack Hays should be told about it. Why hadn't they done so instead of just talking? Marching up from Guerrero along another *camino real.* Why, there was no telling how close they were to San

Antonio right now! The history of 1836 might be repeated.

"I've got to warn 'em," Joel said through gritted teeth. "There may be time to do something yet."

Consuela's heart skipped a beat. "You mean leave me? You mean go to Bexar and help the Texians fight off the Mexicans?"

"I danged sure do," he snapped. "We're nowhere near ready to fight a regular army. I reckon we're worse off than in '36. You know how many men Hays has? Maybe fifty. Fifty men! This army you're talking about can gobble 'em up before they know what's going on."

"But, Joel," she protested, "you can't just ride off and—"

He didn't hear her. "We can raise the men, all right. Nobody's about to whip Texas with three thousand men. But it'll take time. They'll have to come from Goliad and Columbia and even Nacogdoches. They'll come in droves from the United States, too. But they won't get here by September."

Consuela caught his arm. "Joel, listen to me," she begged. "Think about me for a minute. You can't leave me here alone. Let soldiers fight the war if there must be one. You have much to do here. You haven't finished the cabin. You haven't cleared any land. And how can I live here without you? Merciful God, Joel, I can't live here alone!"

She didn't move him.

"You can get by," he said. "You got to. I can't hide from my duty."

"Your duty is to me, too. You brought me here. You can't desert me."

He shook his shaggy head, and tried to explain.

"I'm not deserting you, honey. I'll scoot back just as soon as I can."

"How soon will that be? Two days? Two weeks?"

Joel groaned. How did he know? How could he even guess until he had learned about the seriousness of this Mexican menace?

"It all depends," he said. "This plot might turn out to be another windy. There's been more than one." He went on. Other rumored invasions hadn't amounted to a hill of beans. But if Santa Anna had indeed sent a French general north with a sizeable army, then it could turn out to be a real scrap. They'd fight the invaders as fiercely as in 1836, falling back when they had to, but never giving up.

Tears streamed down Consuela's cheeks. How could he stand there and talk of leaving her for weeks and months?

What else could he do? Desperation strained his voice, made him sound hoarse and gruff. How had Santa Anna been beaten the first time? By Texians staying home to improve their cabins and clear their lands, or by volunteers rallying around Sam Houston?

"But what about me?" Consuela wailed.

She wouldn't be the first woman left at home while her husband went off to fight, answered Joel. Other women had gotten along; so could she. The next morning he'd hang more meat up to dry and cure. His father had gone off to fight under Andrew Jackson in the Creek War, leaving him alone with his grandmother, and she had managed. No use of Consuela carrying on any more. His duty was to warn the rangers, and then pitch in to help with the fighting. And that's what he was going to do.

Consuela bent her head and bit her lips. Her tears were wasted; she might as well save them until he had gone. For he was certainly going.

He worked feverishly the next morning. He hung two deer carcasses up to cure. He cut a large stack of firewood. He showed her how to handle his long-barreled rifle. He couldn't be sure how much attention she was paying him, but he schooled her as well as he could in so short a time. He kept hoping she would get into a better humor, but she didn't. She lifted cold lips to kiss him goodbye and all she said before he rode off was that she hoped she could be there when he returned. But she didn't promise it. At the time she didn't see how it was possible.

Chapter Nine

Manuel Canales left Agua Dulce in the midst of the hulabaloo about Consuela's disappearance. His timetable was running short. He had three more *proprietors* to solicit and then to personally confirm the lack of fortifications in San Antonio.

He departed without explaining the dead bodies of his retinue. Don Carlo`s, grieved and stunned by his granddaughter's disappearance, thought the corpses of small interest. Apparently the Texians had killed them, though no one suggested any motive. And no one bothered to guess why the soldiers were out of uniform. With Consuela missing, nothing else mattered.

Manuel had told some of what he knew. Consuela had slipped out of the hacienda to meet the Gringo, Joel Howard. Had she eloped or been kidnapped? The distressed Don Carlos could not imagine anything but the latter. It was incon-ceivable to him that Consuela would leave volun-tarily without extra clothing or personal effects. In a rage Don Carlos demanded that Ewen Cameron take his crew and depart. The Scot obeyed. What else could he do with this *proprietor*'s armcd vaqueros surrounding his camp?

Canales hurried so on his business that he didn't brood much about Consuela's fate. His personal guess was that she had gone willingly, but it didn't suit him to defend a Texian in any way. Maybe Don Carlos would change his mind and contribute to Santa Anna's war chest.

The next *proprietor* contributed ten thousand *pesos*. Manuel rode on toward San Antonio in civilian clothes. He had filled his purse. Now to scout the Texian defenses. No one challenged him as he rode up to the Alamo Plaza and dismounted.

Here, according to his uncle, the campaign of 1836 had been lost. The Texians had resisted siege for thirteen long years. They had taken a sickening toll of Santa Anna's best soldiers. That delay had enabled cannon to reach Texas from the United States. Santa Anna didn't intend to pay such a high price for San Antonio again. This time the town must be taken by surprise.

The city's population was still more Spanish than American. Manuel attracted little attention as he moved about. There was no hint of any plan for defense of the town. Major Hays' rangers were stationed at a camp some twelve miles away. Canales questioned merchants of known loyalty to Mexico and heard from them that the time was ripe. San Antonio sprawled drowsily in the sun, ready to be taken.

The *Yanquis* in the vicinity? There might be a

hundred ready to fight, certainly no more. They were drifters mostly, coarse and rowdy men. Manuel nodded. Were Texians ever anything else?

He moved from one grogshop to another, making mental note of everything he overheard. Mostly these Texians cursed the government, the weather, the Comanches and the way German immigrants were acquiring the choicest tracts of public land.

In a saloon directly across from the Alamo, Canales came face to face with a familiar Texian. Manuel couldn't place the man for a moment. Where, he wondered, had he seen this broad-shouldered bullnecked man before? Suddenly Manuel remembered. This was the *Yanqui* who had fought Joel Howard at Agua Dulce. The way the squat American held his right hand convinced Canales. And the burly Frenchman drinking with him—he had been with Ewen Cameron, too.

"Pardon," Manuel said politely, "but I believe I have seen you before."

Jared Applegate surveyed him with an unfriendly scowl.

"Yeah? What if you have?"

"Weren't you involved in a fight with another Texian at Agua Dulce?"

"I could have been," Jared said sourly, "if that's any of your business."

Canales kept his temper under control. He

remembered that in a short time his dragoons would be slaughtering such uncouth men at every opportunity.

"My name is Manuel Canales," he said. "I am eager for information about the hombre you fought—*Senor* Howard."

Jared shook his head. "I ain't. I don't wanna see him again unless I'm looking at him over a gunsight."

Manuel nodded. He had hoped the bullnecked man held a bitter grudge.

"I would be most happy to buy the wine," Canales said, "if you will tell me what you know about this *Senor* Howard."

Jared cocked his head. "How about tequila?"

"Whatever you wish."

Applegate grinned at Boulain. "Come on, Frenchy. We ain't got nothing to lose."

The two gringos sat at Manuel's table. When Canales ordered tequila for them Jared added his own instructions.

"Just bring a whole bottle," he said.

Then, pushing back in his chair and squinting at the Spaniard, Jared demanded: "What do you wanna know about Howard, and why?"

"Just after your fight with *Senor* Howard—after you left—he kidnapped the granddaughter of Don Carlos. She was my betrothed."

"The hell you say! Hear that, Frenchy? The button grabbed a Mex wench for himself."

"No wench," snapped Canales, "but *Senorita* Consuela O'Rourke."

Jared's shrug showed how little that impressed him.

"You must know something about *Senor* Howard. Have you heard of him since?"

"Nope. He never was a side-kick of mine. Or Frenchy's either. Cowtailed to Ewen too much to suit us."

"You don't know anything about him?"

"Oh, some," Jared said carelessly. "He located some land on the Medina somewhere, I know that. Drove some cows there a year or so back and put up a cabin." He refilled his glass. "He mighta took the wench there. But that's just a guess."

Manuel nodded. He considered it a valid lead.

"Where is this land? How far from here?"

"Sixty miles mebbe. I dunno where exactly. But it ain't too far from Helena."

Canales' eyes went from Jared to the Frenchman and back again. The Spaniard was positive he hadn't misjudged either man.

"Do you suppose you could find it?"

"If we was looking for it," Jared said calmly, "which we ain't. And which we ain't apt to do."

"Not even if it's worth your while?"

Applegate studied Canales, then grinned. "That's a hoss of a different color. Me and Frenchy can do a lot of things when it suits us."

"This should suit you. It's worth money to have

the *Senorita* O'Rourke returned to her grand-father. And for *Senor* Howard to get his just deserts."

"What do you mean, his deserts?"

"Bring his ears to Agua Dulce," Manuel said. "That's the custom of my people—to pay a bounty for a scoundrel's ears."

"I getcha," murmured Applegate. He held up his right hand, demonstrating its stiffness. "Howard ruined me as a fighter. I reckon you know that."

"You can still shoot, can't you? And you could return the *Senorita* O'Rourke to her grandfather after rescuing her from that scoundrel?"

"Oh, sure," said Jared, pouring another drink. "But you're talking risky business, friend. This Howard ain't no sitting duck. He got a pair of five-shooters from Sam Walker and he knows how to use 'em. I ain't about to mess around with him."

"How about a thousand *pesos*?"

Jared's eyes flickered and Canales knew he had impressed the man. "A thousand *pesos* for the return of the *Senorita* O'Rourke to her grand-father," Manuel said slowly, "and another thousand for *Senor* Howard's ears."

"Make it two thousand," Applegate said a little hoarsely.

"I'll meet you halfway. Two thousand *pesos* for the *senorita*, a thousand for killing Howard."

As Jared scowled, Manuel went on. "But the *Senorita* O'Rourke is more important than the other. You'll be paid nothing without her safe return."

"I getcha," grunted Jared. "You're more worried about the wench."

"I intend to marry her," Manuel said stiffly.

Applegate fingered his glass. "How'd we collect? I danged sure ain't trusting you for it."

Canales thought quickly. "I'll leave the money with Don Carlos. You'll be paid by him. In gold, too."

Jared looked to Boulain.

"What do you say, Frenchy?"

"It's worth something in advance," Boulain said cautiously. "What do you call it—a token payment."

"Yeah," said Jared quickly. "We need some eating money while we're scouting around."

"A hundred *pesos* each," proposed Canales, opening his waistcoat. "That should defray your expenses."

"It'd help," conceded Jared. He took a deep breath. "Mister," he said grimly, "you got yourself a deal. Ain't he, Frenchy?"

"With me," Pierre said with a shrug, "it's only the money. I don't know how we can make three thousand pesos any easier."

Canales paid over the agreed advance and left San Antonio immediately. He considered his trip highly successful. He could report back that the town was without defenses. He'd encountered no actual risks, but his feat would assume heroic proportions anyhow. And he'd set two unscrupulous gringos on the trail of Joel Howard and Consuela. Now to double back by Agua Dulce and cement his ties with Don Carlos.

Garza listened gravely to Manuel's account. "You have done well," he said. "At least, you have done something. And I—I've only wrung my hands and grieved."

"I won't rest until I rescue her from that *Yanqui*," Manuel said coldly. "And when I do, I want her as my wife."

Garza bent his head. "You shall have her," he promised. "This time I will make the decision."

Consuela looked after Joel until he was swallowed up in the timber. Then, sobbing, she hurried to the refuge of her chapel. Kneeling before the polished cedar cross, she poured out her self-pity. A long prayer relieved her fears. Joel could not have done anything else. He was a Texian; he had realized his duty and hadn't hesitated. Her duty was clear, too. Dread it all she might, she must take care of herself until his return.

She began the ordeal with determination. The best way to endure the loneliness was to stay busy. She finished piecing together the buckskin shirt. It fitted snugly; her first hint that she was gaining weight. She was actually thriving among these hardships.

Soap to make, corn to shell, curing skins to smoke, her own meals to cook—she easily occupied herself from daylight to dark. The nights, though, were something else. At first she couldn't sleep a wink. She found it easier to doze in the daytime than to relax in the awful darkness. But that fear gradually lessened. Soon she was sleeping fitfully until the sun vaulted over the pecans and oaks to hit squarely on the cabin walls.

She kept Joel's rifle close at hand, though she had no intention of ever using it. In the first place, she was scared of the weapon. It might go off in her face instead of throwing its deadly load at a target. And, second, Consuela blanched at the thought of killing a sleek, handsome deer. She didn't even want to shoot an ugly, grunting javelina.

Noises in the timber—there were so many of them that she trained herself to ignore them all. So if Jared Applegate and Pierre Boulain had given any warning, she wouldn't have noticed it. Probably they didn't. They'd been muskrat trappers along the Sabine and Neches before their fling with Cameron's cowboys. Both were cautious, stealthy hunters. And both had a wholesome respect for Joel Howard's shooting. Neither showed himself until certain that the tall, copper-haired man was nowhere about.

Then Jared darted out of the brush to seize Consuela from behind. She screamed and whirled to claw at him. Her fingernails raked his unshaved face and Jared cursed in pain and anger.

He smashed his clenched fist against her temple and Consuela dropped without another sound. Boulain, charging a few strides behind his bull-necked companion, knelt over her.

She was all right, he said in relief. But it was a wonder.

"She's a woman," the Frenchman snapped. "Don't hit her like that again."

"She's a bearcat," growled Jared, feeling his shallow, stinging wounds. "She danged near scratched my eyes out."

His eyes gleamed as he studied the unconscious girl. "She's a looker, ain't she?" he gloated.

"She is a beautiful woman," Boulain agreed. He looked around at the unimpressive clearing. "Too beautiful for the woods and a log cabin," he added. "We are doing right to take her back to her grandfather."

"Yeah," grinned Jared, "and we're getting paid for it."

He strode into the cabin and returned with one of Joel's riatas. Hidden in the brush, the two had already planned how they would handle their captive. Jared knotted the riata around Consuela's waist while Boulain bridled and saddled the mare. Next they helped themselves to meat, sourdough, beans, fruit and blankets. They moved swiftly, for there was no telling when Howard would return. For all they knew he might be working cattle nearby, perhaps he had gone to Helena after more supplies. Certainly they meant to waste no time getting away from the Medina.

Consuela groaned and opened her eyes. Jared jerked her to her feet.

"Come on, lady bird," he ordered. "Your hoss is waiting for you."

"No!" she cried, shrinking away from him. "Merciful God, no."

Applegate brandished his fist. "You want another dose of knuckles?"

Boulain moved in behind Consuela and caught her shoulders.

"Don't fight us," he advised gently. "Don't force us to beat you into submission and tie you hand and foot."

She faced him hopefully. Pierre was rough-looking enough but she took heart at his calm voice.

"What are you going to do with me?"

"Take you back to your grandfather," he said soothingly. "That is all. There's a reward for your return and we mean to collect it."

Her eyes went from him to Jared Applegate.

"And that's—that's all?"

Boulain nodded. "It's the money, 'mselle." A light gleamed in his eyes. "I am somewhat of a rascal, *mon cheri*. Fate has made me so. But you are safe with us until you reach your grandfather's rancho."

Consuela let him help her up on the mare. It was folly to resist. Joel, she mused, must risk Don Carlos' wrath, after all. If, that was, he ever got her back.

Chapter Ten

It was no false alarm Joel took to San Antonio. Across the Frio River and the little used *camino real* came General Adrian Woll's army, an awesome sight. First came the dragoons in their colorful blue and white garb, their lances glistening in the sun. Next marched a segment of infantry, men moving in perfect step and from a distance appearing as peas in a pod. Then rolled the twelve pieces of artillery, bright, gleaming fieldpieces. Right behind lumbered the supply wagons, mostly *carretas*, and a few carriages. Other smart units of cavalry and infantry brought up the rear.

San Antonio and Texas were alerted, thanks to the tall copper-haired young giant who had galloped into Jack Hays' camp and told a convincing story. Captain Hays had wasted no time checking the rumor. With ten rangers and Joel Howard as a guide, the ranger leader had galloped headlong into Woll's advance patrols south of the Frio. For nearly fifteen minutes mounted Texians and Mexicans had swapped shots before Hays pulled his men out of the fight. Their responsibility was to let Texas know the enemy was coming, not to try to stop the Frenchman themselves.

It was a lively little scrap, though. Joel Howard's blood tingled every time he thought of it. In his battle baptism he'd killed four of the enemy and earned his commanding officer's public approval.

"I brought Howard along to show us the road," Hays said so all of his men could hear. "I didn't know he was going to show us how to fight, too."

"I tried to tell you," Sam Walker said, "but you wouldn't pay me no mind."

Joel grinned, embarrassed but willing to show he was pleased. He'd formed a quick liking for the men of this ranger company, taking to them like he had to Sam. They liked him, too; he knew that by their hoo-rahing.

They'd tangled with a Mexican patrol at the Atascosita, too, this time with Hays' company at full strength. The forty-odd rangers had wiped out a detail of sixteen dragoons without a casualty. Then Hays had divided his group again. Walker and twelve others were ordered to keep watch on the advancing army. Could he have Howard, too, asked Sam? Hays said if Joel could stand it, he could. So Joel rode with Walker's detail on one circuit after another of Woll's force while Ben McCulloch and the other rangers fanned out in all directions to spread the alarm. Hays himself tried to be everywhere at once. In the same day he conferred with San

Antonio's committee of citizens about defense of the town, saw that the first volunteers went into camp on Salado Creek, sent reports to the Secretary of War at Austin and rode back to see how Walker's scouts were faring.

Here Hays came—lickety split, according to Big Foot Wallace, who saw him first. Wallace was a Virginian who towered over Joel by a full three inches. His eyesight was nothing short of remarkable; he identified the two approaching horsemen when Joel saw only faint moving specks in the distance.

Joel hadn't seen enough of the ranger leader to get over being surprised at Hays' unimpressive size and mannerisms. The captain stood no more than five feet nine inches tall and didn't weight over a hundred and fifty pounds dripping wet. He wore a simple homespun shirt and breeches, without even an ornamental kerchief. He spoke in a low even tone and was as sparing with words as his rank allowed. He seemed reluctant to give commands, leaving his lieutenants and enlisted men considerable latitude. All he'd told Walker, for instance, was to keep an eye on the enemy.

"Everything all right?" he asked Sam.

"Well," said Sam, nodding in the direction of Woll's army, "we ain't stopped 'em yet, Jack."

This slim commander was "Jack" to most of his men, "Cap" to the others. Joel had addressed him as "Mister Hays" a time or two and had been reprimanded.

Hays stared at the Mexicans. "Nope," he agreed, "they're still coming." He shifted his weight and took off his soft-brimmed hat to wipe sweat from his forehead. "Not much chance of us stopping 'em this side of San Antonio, either."

"Why not?" demanded Sam. "There's about fifteen hundred of 'em. Give us four hundred volunteers and we can hold 'em here 'til Kingdom Come. Ain't help coming?"

"It's coming," Jack said, "but slow. Caldwell is camped on the Salado now. Marched most of the night to get there. He has a hundred men, maybe. Ewen Cameron is supposed to be right behind him. And Ben McCulloch sent back word that a company is forming at Bastrop."

The captain turned suddenly to Joel. "While I think of it, Howard—you want to join your old bunch?"

Joel hesitated. Hays meant Ewen, of course. The Scot would have his brushpoppers ready for fight. But, according to what Preacher Scott had told him at Helena, Cameron was still miffed because Don Carlos had broken up their hunt on Agua Dulce Creek. Besides, Joel saw no reason to abandon his present companions.

"I'm doing all right here," he said.

Hays' eyes twinkled. "You sure are. Keep Sam straight and you're worth your weight in gold."

114

Hays put back on his hat. "Well, back to town for more palaver," he said a little disgustedly. "Another committee meeting." His eyes roved over them, twinkling. "Don't you galoots start anything you can't finish," he warned. "We'll save our didoes until later."

"We ain't doing a thing," said Sam. "Just watching 'em."

But late that afternoon Sam himself set a reckless example for the others. The rangers circled around Woll's army without being seen. From another live oak thicket they watched the Mexicans prepare for bivouac. The several tents raised brought disdainful snorts from men who slept on the ground more often than not. The rangers boasted no sort of supply vehicle; each man had his own blanket, some sweetened ground corn in his wallet and a slicker rolled up behind his saddle. He ate or slept when the chance came and how he did either was his own worry.

"Let 'em have their tents," grunted Chevaille. "Mebbe we'll catch Woll asleep in his—like we did Santa Anna."

Then the sharp-eyed Wallace called Walker's attention to the platoon leaving the Mexican camp. Woll had selected a level plain for his camp site; Big Foot guessed that these foot soldiers were going after firewood.

"If it's a hot time they want," grinned Sam, "we'll oblige 'em."

He spurred his black horse down the slope. His followers needed no orders; they galloped right behind him. Sam led them around a ridge which concealed them from their quarry for the time being. The Mexicans were after firewood, sure enough; most of them carried axes. A handful of snappily clad dragoons rode in escort.

Joel realized Sam's strategy. Walker meant to charge the Mexicans from an angle, cutting them off from the main camp. If the ruse worked, they'd claim several victims before reinforcements hurried out. Joel could have taken the lead; his chestnut was faster than Walker's gelding. But he held back, riding even with dark-bearded Mike Chevaille and Big Foot. Wallace rode a mule, claiming no horse was stout enough to carry him all day. However, his long-eared mount gave away little in fleetness. Wallace was close enough to fire the first shot with his heavy double-barreled rifle. He hit his mark, too, and started the Mexicans scurrying for cover. The enemy dragoons rode forward as if to make a stand but broke ranks when Sam, Joel and Chevaille opened fire with their five-shooters. The repeating pistols were too much for the lancers. What chance did they have against horsemen who carried ten shots apiece and could reload at a gallop?

Whooping, the rangers pursued the dragoons to within a half-mile of their camp, then wheeled around to annihilate the stragglers. Cannon balls screamed after them but they were untouched. A half-hour later they dismounted a safe distance from Woll's overwhelming numbers and gloated over their success. They had killed ten or twelve on this foray, anyhow. More important, of course, was the effect on Mexican morale. The invaders would never get a chance to relax this side of the Rio Grande.

Two hours later, as pitch-darkness closed in, Walker and Chevaille tested the Mexican watch. It was strong enough. After a few hurried shots the two rangers galloped back to the live oaks.

The Texians posted no sentries themselves. Without fires, sleeping scattered about, no formal watch was necessary. The rangers simply spread their blankets and fell sound asleep almost at once.

But not Joel. He dozed off a time or two but not for long. He couldn't get Consuela out of his thoughts. How long since he had left her? Five nights—no, six. He'd ridden hard and reached San Antonio in late afternoon. Learning the rangers were camped on the San Antonio River, not in town, he'd left Bexar without gratifying his curiosity about such places as the Alamo, the Governor's Palace or the dance halls where smiling *senoritas* taught the fandango for modest fees. He'd found Jack Hays easily enough and told his story. At daylight he'd left with Hays to verify what Consuela had told him.

Everything she'd said was true. The war was on again after a lapse of six years. There was no telling how long the fighting would last, either. There might be other armies coming in Woll's wake—probably were, for surely Santa Anna didn't expect to reconquer Texas with only fifteen hundred men. The Texians had killed and captured that many at San Jacinto in 1836. If volunteers rallied to Hays' help as expected, Texas would have two thousand men in the field in a week's time.

Even so, mused Joel, he'd be away from the Medina another two or three weeks. Could Consuela stand it alone that long? She might with the comfort of her small chapel and her daily prayers.

He turned over on his side and closed his eyes. He wanted to get this business over with and hurry back to his dark-haired bride.

Chapter Eleven

His spirits rose as daylight came and the rangers resumed their heckling. This type of fighting suited Joel, and he suited it. A few others in Walker's detail had managed to get Colt repeating pistols; those so armed bore the brunt of the skirmishes. And several times the Texian horsemen charged down upon lancer details. As hecklers these rangers were unequaled anywhere.

The invaders stopped three miles from San Antonio, pitching camp on the river near the San Juan mission. Jack Hays rode up during the night with the rest of his company. The captain brought fresh meat and beans; Walker's men ate their first full meal in four days. The Texian volunteer army was organizing across the Salado, Hays said. They'd chosen Matthew Caldwell as their commanding officer. Was Hays disappointed? If so, Joel couldn't tell it. But his men were and minced no words about it, Joel included. In these few days he'd come to share the company's general feeling for this quiet-spoken captain. Hays could take a handful of riders and get a lot done. Who was Caldwell? A veteran Texas Indian fighter, sure, the hero of Plum Creek; Joel knew that as well as anybody. But Caldwell was a soldier of the old school. He thought of an army in terms of foot soldiers, backwoodsmen with rifles hiding behind a barricade—as Andy Jackson had fought at New Orleans. He didn't know beans about quick, unexpected sallies on horseback.

But he was commander-in-chief; from here on the rangers were under his orders.

The Mexicans made no move to break camp the next morning. Instead, about nine o'clock, a trio of lancers crossed the river with a flag of truce. Hays rode to meet them alone. The rangers watching from the slope jeered at the exchange of courtesies. Look at Jack bowing and scraping! Why didn't he just put a slug in the Mexican colonel while he had the chance?

The parley was brief, the Mexican trio recrossing the river and Hays returning to his amused ranks.

Woll offered to spare the town if he encountered no resistance, Hays said. The Mexicans would allow a reasonable time for reply before advancing nearer.

Off galloped Hays to inform both General Caldwell and the Citizens Committee of San Antonio. The rangers rested their horses under shade trees and waited glumly for their leader's return.

"It's like this every danged time," raged Mike Chevaille. "We can beat 'em in a battle but they outtalk us. Honorable surrender, hell! There ain't no such thing to a Mexican." He pointed to

"Slats" Hardin, a rangy, thin-lipped ranger who seldom had a word to say. "Tell 'em about it, Slats," demanded Mike. "You were at Goliad. You know what honorable terms mean to a Mexican."

Joel looked at Hardin curiously. He hadn't known that about Slats. Only twenty-six men out of five hundred had survived the Goliad massacre. A man who had lived through it must have strong feelings about flags of truce and gentlemanly negotiations.

"I just fight," shrugged Hardin. "When I'm told and where I'm told. The high monkety-monks—they do the palavering."

Hays came back about noon. One look at his face told the rangers what had been decided. They remounted and circled around the town to reach Salado Creek, several miles to the southeast. As far as Bexar was concerned, Woll could "help himself to the mustard." This time there would not be another Alamo.

Into San Antonio marched Woll's orderly army, preceded by a brass band. But the discouraged rangers took heart when they reached Salado Creek and saw for themselves how the Texian volunteers were organized for battle.

General Caldwell himself came to visit Hays' campfires. He had almost three hundred men ready. Woll would have a tough time crossing the Salado, he promised. He wanted the rangers to intercept any cavalry detail sent out to reconnoiter the surrounding country. The Texians could make Woll's conquest of Bexar a hollow victory. What harm could the Frenchman do if they kept him bottled up between the San Antonio River and Salado Creek? Cut off from all communications, unable to gauge the strength of his opposition, he might find his position unbearable.

"Sounds good to me," Walker grunted as Caldwell left. "Somebody's showing some hoss sense."

The next morning, while his men ate breakfast, Hays talked long and earnestly with Caldwell and Ewen Cameron. Their final agreement apparently suited Jack; the young captain's face showed it. Ewen looked several times in Joel's direction but showed no friendliness. Joel finally decided to ignore the Scot's distant manner. Ewen had been his friend and tutor. He could thank Cameron for the land and cattle he owned and the gold he wore under his shirt.

"Howdy, Ewen," he ventured.

Cameron's eyes met his squarely. "How are you, lad?"

"Bueno." Joel shifted his weight. "Sorry about that deal at Agua Dulce, Ewen. I put you to a heap of trouble."

"Don't waste your sympathies on me," the Scot said crisply. "I haven't a Mexican wife hanging around my neck like a millstone. Or have you come to your senses and sent her back to her people?"

"I haven't," Joel said, "and I'm not."

Ewen nodded. "You will, or she'll leave you on her own. There's no mixing such different races and different faiths. But you'll have to learn that for yourself."

Cameron turned and walked back to his horse. Joel shook his head and joined the circle of men listening to Hays. There was no point in letting Ewen's prejudices worry him. He was his own man, not the Scot's. His choice of a wife was his own business.

Hays mentioned nothing about any battle plan agreed upon with Caldwell and Cameron. He only said that the ranger company would redouble its efforts to cut off Woll's communications in any direction. They'd harass San Antonio in three details—his own, Sam Walker's and Ben McCulloch's.

Walker led his troop around the town. By now Woll had artillery set up in the Alamo Plaza. His gunners threw occasional shots at the swiftly moving Texians but no man was hit. Nor, that day, did any lancers come out to challenge them. The next morning the three leaders took their details inside the range of the Frenchman's artillery, gambling that his gunners couldn't hit such swiftly moving targets. They circled daringly within reach of the invaders' carbines.

It took Joel a while to realize the orderly pattern of their apparently reckless riding, but finally it began to make sense. As one troop galloped out of range, another detail swept up.

Any Mexican couriers had to break through the circle of horsemen. Several tried. Joel pursued a lancer on a jet-black horse and shot him out of the saddle. Big Foot Wallace leaped to the ground and carefully searched the dead man despite the bullets raining around him. Wallace found dispatches which Walker sent on to Hays immediately. This report of San Antonio's occupation and Woll's request for further orders would never reach Laredo.

The next day the Mexicans showed signs of cavalry activity themselves. No less than five times Woll sent lancers out after the Texians. They came rather cautiously, true, halting when the Texian details fell back according to their orders. Hays had his sound reason for avoiding small skirmishes. Sooner or later the Frenchman must send out his cavalry for a full-scale clash. The ranger captain waited patiently. So did Caldwell's volunteer force, now in battle station on this side of the creek.

Not so the ranger rank and file. They couldn't understand these orders, so they didn't like them. As Chevaille said, they were riding their butts sore and their horses out. They were using up everything except their powder.

The strain was telling on General Woll and his officers, too. All sorts of rumors reached the Frenchman about Texian volunteers marching toward Bexar. Woll couldn't analyze his own position. Had he fashioned his own trap? Were the Texians quietly surrounding San Antonio and intending to assault the city when they had gained superior numbers? Another Mexican general, Martin Perfecto de Cos, had capitulated here in 1836, surrendering costly material as well as one thousand two hundred seasoned troops.

Woll finally decided to send out his cavalry. He couldn't move out in any direction until these rangers had been squelched.

He sent the pick of his dragoons with an artillery unit close behind. First, the lancers tried to bottle up Hays. The ranger led his detail away. McCulloch's group moved over to join Hays and then Walker's, after Ad Gillespie had raced over with orders. Walker came eagerly, his dozen followers right behind him. This might be the fight they had been waiting for.

Instead, Hays ordered them to fall back. The lancers came across the plain in eager attack. Hays and Walker led their men in what appeared to be headlong flight, leaving McCulloch and ten others to make a show of resistance, as if protecting a retreat. Woll's dragoons pressed them hard, following the

Texians into the timber along Salado Creek.

Three hundred rifles cracked, with the nattily uniformed men as targets. The bold Mexican assault turned into panic. Hays, seeing the enemy's confusion, whirled his company around. Into the milling ranks of dragoons they charged, five-shooters blazing, bowie knives flashing. The cannon did the invaders no good at all. Caldwell's volunteers were screened by the timber and the artillerymen did not dare turn their sights onto the tangle of rangers and lancers. Joel fired his ten shots, hurried to reload. A lance grazed his shoulder. Out of the corner of his eye he saw Sam Walker grappling with a dragoon. Both men toppled to the ground and the Mexican raised his saber. Joel swung his five-shooters and riddled the lancer. Walker swung up on the dead man's horse; his own had been shot out from under him.

The lancers broke into disorderly flight. Caldwell's infantrymen had stormed out of the brush now and their withering fire took some toll of the fleeing Mexicans. But the rangers killed more. Woll's gunners scrambled to get back into town with their cannon. Their bold effort to rout Hays' company ended in bloody defeat. They left fifty of their number dead, and as many more staggered into San Antonio with wounds.

The rangers pursued the enemy to within a half-mile of the Alamo, then fell back as Woll's artillery opened up. Dismounting, the Texians began stripping the Mexican corpses of all valuables. Big Foot Wallace even pulled off a dead lancer's trousers. Spurs, sabers, rings and charms—the rangers took what they pleased. Some of the bodies yielded silver and gold coins. Thinking about Consuela, Joel appropriated several gaudy sashes. Then he realized how horrified she would be to learn how they were gotten and turned them over to Kit Acklin.

He felt a little nauseated as he tethered his tired chestnut and joined Sam, Big Foot and others around a supper fire. He couldn't glory too much in his first real battle. Was a massacre anything to rejoice about? Maybe, he mused, he had not learned to hate the Mexicans as most Texians did. He sighed and stretched out on his back. He hoped he never developed a bitterness like Ewen Cameron's. He was willing to despise some Spaniards as individuals—Manuel Canales, for instance. But he didn't want to hate them as a people. He had been impressed by Carlos Garza to start with and meant to be respectful of the *proprietor* again. He'd take Consuela to beg the Don's forgiveness and solemnize their marriage if and when this invasion was beaten back.

And that wouldn't be too long. The Texians were in high spirits. They'd bared their teeth and gained an overwhelming victory. Woll would think several times before ordering another assault. Chances were this war would be over in a week or two. Joel sighed again. He hoped so. It seemed as if he had been separated from Consuela forever.

The setback aggravated Woll's uncertainties. He'd lost the strength of a full company, and his picked cavalry at that. Worse still, he'd learned nothing about the numbers of the Texian army. His dazed lieutenants weren't sure whether they had charged into two hundred men or two thousand. All they knew was that suddenly the woods had belched out sheets of rifle fire, stopping them dead in their tracks.

Woll decided that discretion was the better part of valor. Lopez de Santa Anna had made it clear that a debacle like San Jacinto must be avoided. Woll collected his artillery and supply wagons and marched out of San Antonio unexpectedly. His columns were already moving along the *real* to Laredo before the Texians realized what he was about.

Caldwell ordered the rangers to resume their forays, but for once Hays was slow to obey. His men were tired, he said, and their horses spent. Besides, Woll might be planning some sort of flanking maneuver.

The Texians rested for two days, then moved after the retreating Mexicans. Woll's force was easy to overtake, for the invaders could travel no faster than their artillery. The rangers were heckling the Frenchman's flanks again before he'd gained the Hondo River.

An early autumn flood had sent that stream on the rise. Hays proposed to Caldwell, Cameron and other commanders that the Texians attack during the river crossing. The Texian force had grown to five hundred men, enough for a full-scale battle. Let Woll get half of his army across, said Hays, then strike.

Caldwell seemed convinced. Word swept through the Texian ranks that the crucial battle was coming up. The men rolled in their blankets that night sure of another San Jacinto the next day. But they awoke to find Woll prepared for any such assault. During the night he'd set up a formidable battery on the north bank to protect his crossing. Caldwell called his staff officers into a hurried huddle.

The conference wasn't held in a private tent, or even a secluded spot, but out in the open. The leader of each company had his opinion and he didn't mind expressing it. The rank and file wasn't ordered back; all who pressed close enough could hear almost every word. Second-hand reports of what this man said and that one opposed, spread like wildfire. Walker's troop, disgustedly waiting a half-mile upstream from Woll's battery, got almost a word-for-word account of the parley.

Hays and Cameron wanted to wipe out the Mexican battery and then fight as planned. Most others didn't. And Matthew Caldwell—"Old Paint"—was undecided.

"Trouble with us," griped Big Foot, "is that we got too many chiefs and not enough Indians."

"Too many yellowbellies, too," said Mike. "Just the sight of a cannon scares 'em stiff."

Hays offered to lead his rangers against the artillery emplacement. His men would draw the first fusillade, then tie up the gunners in hand-to-hand fighting. Let Caldwell or Cameron bring up a hundred men to reinforce his position and they'd capture Woll's cannon, and shell the Frenchman's crossing with his own artillery. You oughta hear Jack, said Kit Acklin, bringing word for Walker's unit to stand by. You never heard him throw his weight around like that. Danged if he couldn't outshout any of 'em.

Here came their captain, his argument won. He was his terse, quiet-spoken, usual self again. They could see what they had to do as well as he. They'd feint a flanking maneuver, then go at the battery lickety-split. The Mexicans would over-shoot them, he said, gesturing his rangers into their saddles.

Joel licked his dry lips as he rode behind Walker. Charge right into blazing cannon—he'd never done that before. He wanted to agree with Hays; so far, Woll's impressive fieldpieces hadn't hurt anybody. All the shot hurled into the Salado timber had amounted to just so much noise. Still—he couldn't help being uneasy about it. No reason to deny it, he was just plain scared. He felt weak inside, a trifle nauseated. He'd felt that way after shooting his way out of Canales' ambush and realizing what he had done.

Then he had no time to worry about how he felt. The ranger company veered toward the Mexican cannon at a casual gait. From the distance of a half-mile they appeared to be starting a careless swing around the river ford. But at Hays' signal the entire company went galloping forward. Spurs raked quick-starting mustangs into a dead run. Lying low over their horses' necks, the rangers charged at the battery.

Cannon roared; shot and shell screamed out. But in the split seconds between orders to fire and actual explosion Woll's gunners lost the range. The onrushing men came faster than they had expected. The artillery blasts burst over the Texians' heads. And there was no time to reload. Hays, Walker and McCulloch tumbled from their saddles and scrambled over the earthen barricade. Nearly fifty whooping men came after them. Some of Woll's gunners tried to fight back, the others fled.

For a minute or two the rangers held the battery; but for no longer than that. Every Mexican soldier who hadn't crossed the river came rushing to recapture the cannon. And the Texian reinforcements hadn't even started.

Hays looked at the oncoming enemy, then back at his own lines. He acted instantly, scrambling out of the redoubt and ordering his men to follow. The rangers recovered their mustangs and galloped away from the hail of carbine bullets. Something hot seared Joel's hip and he might have fallen without Big Foot's steadying hand.

Hays signaled a halt when they were at a safe distance. His usually impassive face was as dark as a thundercloud.

"What'll we do now, Jack?" asked McCulloch.

"I don't know," snapped Hays, "and I don't care."

With that he turned and rode toward Caldwell's ranks.

Later, sitting glumly by a small fire while Acklin broiled venison, Hays denied saying anything to "Old Paint." "What was there to say?" Jack demanded. He didn't stop the jawing of his men but he wouldn't listen to it. He leaped to his feet and stalked off.

Most of the rangers chuckled after him. They weren't the type to brood over lost opportunities. And it amused them to see their leader so riled.

Caldwell's excuses circulated everywhere. Some of his captains claimed they'd never agreed to the attack in the first place. Another said the terrain between his station and the battery was too wet; his men would have never reached the fighting in time. A separate version came from the Bastrop company. Hays should have held back until the rest of them were ready. His quick sally had caught them by surprise, too.

If Jack Hays had said nothing immediately after the retreat, he said it later. He was disgusted with such disorganized leadership. He was exercising his own prerogatives of individual command now. The rest of the Texians could trail Woll to the Rio Grande if they wished; he was taking his company back to San Antonio to await orders from President Sam Houston. Let Houston appoint a commander-in-chief and organize a regular army. Hays wanted no part of any more fighting with each captain making his own decisions.

Some hot words flew. The Bastrop leader pointed out that his men hadn't volunteered to fight a war. They'd hurried to help out on Salado Creek, nothing more. Most of them had ridden away from home on a minute's notice. They had their families and farms to look after. They weren't supposed to be full-time soldiers and his bunch was pulling out for home.

Others voiced the same sentiments. Joel kept his own counsel among the disgruntled rangers. He had to agree it was a damned shame that they hadn't wiped out Woll's army while they had the chance. But he couldn't bemoan the termination of the campaign. Like the men from Bastrop and Gonzales, he wanted to get home.

Chapter Twelve

Consuela was gone! Joel had a premonition of that as he reached the clearing and she was nowhere in sight. He flung back the deerskin flap and saw that the cabin had not been used in several days. The dress she'd worn away from Agua Dulce lay draped across one of the benches. Apparently she'd left in her loose-fitting blouse and buckskin skirt.

The same rain which had flooded the Hondo River had struck here, completely obliterating any tell-tale tracks or signs. The mare was gone, too. Everything else was just as he'd left it. No, someone had almost exhausted the supply shelf.

Joel dropped onto the rough bench and stared at the dirt floor. She was gone. He was sure where, too—back to her grandfather. She'd endured the loneliness and hardships long enough. He could imagine her emerging from one of her prayer sessions, saddling the horse and starting for Agua Dulce Creek with few qualms about the risk. She'd almost done it once before. How had she dismissed any fears then? If God wanted her to go, then God would see that she got there safely.

Joel heaved a deep sigh. He hoped God had.

He'd have to find out if she had gotten home safely; he'd never rest easily until he knew. But he'd never go after her. How could he doubt that she had done the right thing? Certainly Ewen Cameron would say so. Ewen, in fact, had predicted this. The Scot's stern words came back to Joel. There was no happy fusion of such widely different nationalities and faiths. Joel hadn't believed it. He'd pitied Ewen a little for holding such a bitter prejudice. He'd been a little repelled by the harsh creed that this country must be Texian or Mexican. If Texas was to hold the land, then Spanish-speaking peoples must be evicted. Not even friendliness was practical, much less intermarriage.

Joel shook his head. He didn't see why that had to be. He would have sworn that Consuela was happy here. Oh, disturbed about their informal way of living together, anxious to regain her grandfather's favor, but happy with Joel—wholeheartedly in love with him. But she hadn't waited for him. What could he believe that would offset the crushing weight of that?

He cut off a slab of the venison and ate without relish. She had pulled out; all he could do was make the best of it. Hays had been disappointed at his leaving; well, shortly, Captain Jack could welcome him back as a full-fledged recruit. For Joel had no intention of hanging around his cabin all winter, even if nothing came of this agitation for a regular army and an invasion of Mexico. If he had no ties anywhere else, he belonged with the rangers. He'd help Sam Walker chase after Comanches if there were no Mexicans to fight. But he hoped a Texian force would march into Mexico. Let 'em spread war through the enemy's country for a while. Let 'em stamp out all resistance along the Rio Grande.

Then, for a moment, his bravado failed him. He could talk big to himself, he could act big. But something was dying on the Medina that night, and Joel knew what it was. A dream, yes, but more. Much more. A part of himself which Consuela O'Rourke hadn't created at all—only destroyed.

The next three months made little sense. And Joel wasn't the only one who felt that way. Every man in the Texian army was complaining.

President Houston had sent them a new commander, General Alex Somervell. He was worse than Caldwell. He led them to Laredo through boggy brush country instead of following the *camino real.* Then he marched south instead of capturing the Mexican outpost.

Now, on December 19, 1842, he had issued the strangest order yet. He announced that he would march his army back to Gonzales and muster out every company.

The army was in an uproar. At least half the

soldiers voiced open defiance. By gum, they weren't about to head back. Hays gave quiet orders to his troop. The rangers must hold down violence. If any of them wanted to cross the river with the demonstrators, then they could go ahead. But there must be no riot.

Joel wasn't sure the rangers could keep order. A committee demanded that Somervell explain his order to the entire ranks. He came willingly, and spoke in an unruffled voice.

"We have neither the power nor the supplies to sustain us in Mexico," he said. "Yesterday I dispatched Major Hays and his ranger company into Guerrero. I demanded five thousand dollars or its equivalent in livestock. Major Hays informs me that most of the citizens have fled, taking their livestock with them. Even if we ransacked every *jacal* in the town, we wouldn't find enough meat to last us three days."

Most eyes looked hopefully to the slim ranger leader. Hays nodded in confirmation of the General's statement.

"We have very little powder," continued Somervell. "We could fight a battle, yes. But we couldn't wage another until we have captured enemy supplies. I feel that time and distance are against us."

A bearded man spoke up from the front ranks, Dick Fisher.

"There are plenty who don't agree, General."

"You are welcome to your opinion, Colonel Fisher," Somervell said crisply. He turned back to the disgusted army. "Most of you volunteered with the understanding that we would invade Mexico. You are free to do so, but not as any official army of the Republic of Texas."

"But, General," protested Tom Green, "that would make us out as sort of free-booters. We ain't that, at all. We just want to take the war to Mexico."

"That is true," conceded Somervell. "But it is also true that Sam Houston has never led or sent a Texas army into certain defeat. Nor, as his appointed general, shall I."

Another demonstration ensued, one of angry disapproval. Fisher finally made himself heard above the uproar.

"Let's get this straight, General. You're turning us loose?"

"Yes."

The General turned and walked away. Fisher waved his hands high.

"Who's for Mexico?" he cried out.

The assents seemed to be in the great majority.

But, noticed Joel, those affirming made a great fuss over it while those intending to return waited quietly. Nearly two hundred decided they had had enough of mock war.

The ranger company took no part in the

demonstration. But when Hays told them to make their choice, most voted for crossing the Rio. Jack wished them luck and left them to organize themselves.

Joel had waited for others to speak first. He had decided for Mexico at once, but hadn't wanted to be a ringleader. Walker was going, and McCulloch and Big Foot.

"First thing," said Sam, "is to name a captain."

Joel licked his lips. "I vote for Sam Walker," he said.

"Nope," Sam said firmly. "Ben is the better man."

"I ain't gonna say that," declared Big Foot. "Why don't you two spit at a crack?"

Thirty-one of the rangers had elected to join Fisher's volunteer force. They elected McCulloch as captain of the rangers in short order.

But there wasn't such unanimity about a commander for the entire force. Sentiment was divided between Fisher and Ewen Cameron. Joel, watching from the fringe of the crowd, sensed that Cameron wanted the command. Joel whispered to Sam and Chevaille and the rangers voted solidly for the Scot. But Fisher won out.

Somervell's followers were already leaving. Hoots followed them, but not from the rangers. Ben quickly showed the same firm leadership as Hays.

• • •

Two days later the Texians camped seven miles downstream from Mier. The stream was wide here, too deep to ford. Boats had to be found before five rangers could reconnoiter the town. Joel scrambled ashore with Walker, Big Foot, Chevaille and Acklin.

Mier, he mused, didn't look like much. It was a different sort of town from San Antonio. The adobe houses adjoined each other facing on a tangle of narrow, crooked streets, all converging on a presidio and central plaza. Nowhere did they see evidence of a garrison. Apparently the five of them could stride right into town without encountering trouble.

Two natives came reluctantly to meet them. Both were frightened men; getting them to answer questions was like squeezing blood out of turnips. One finally admitted to being the alcalde, but mumbled so in giving his name that Joel didn't understand him. But Walker learned enough to convince him that no resistance was in sight. Acklin and Joel went back to the river and signaled to McCulloch. He crossed with most of his company and took charge of negotiations.

Five heavily armed Texians had been enough to frighten Mier's alcalde; twenty-five more nearly paralyzed him. He babbled agreement to McCulloch's demands for supplies. He seemed sure that the Texians meant to slaughter every man, woman and child in the pueblo if he didn't cooperate and Ben didn't correct that impression.

The alcalde routed out other natives and each *jacal* yielded up provisions—dried *cabrito*, beans, maize meal, peppers, gaudy blankets. Finally McCulloch relented. The alcalde's ears were safe for a little while. But the supplies had to be ferried across the river before the deal was closed. When could the alcalde arrange that? He stammered and whined his excuses. The wind kept rising, a norther was certain. His people dared not cross in their small boats. McCulloch nodded. It was indeed getting cold. Tomorrow would be soon enough to deliver the stores. But just to make sure the foodstuffs didn't disappear once the rangers had turned their backs, he'd take *Senor* Alcalde with him as a hostage.

The official trembled but offered no resistance. He spoke to his constituents so rapidly that Joel couldn't understand half of what he said. But no Texian doubted that he exhorted his people to meet the invaders' terms the next morning. This Mexican trembled for his skin.

Joel wished for his slicker as he crouched low in the skiff. The wind was bitterly cold and smack in their faces. Back on the Texas side of the river, he and Sam hustled about to prepare for the cold night. Colonel Fisher had relaxed discipline so that his volunteers could shift for themselves. Most of them had a single blanket. They'd freeze this night without big fires, and these had to be laid so the wind wouldn't send embers flying.

They scooped out recesses in the lee side of a ridge, gathered firewood and huddled together in its warmth. Ben McCulloch was left to sleep with the alcalde. With the taunts of his comrades in his ears, he lay down alongside the Mexican. Joel rolled up in his blanket and pressed closely against Sam. Big Foot's weight bore against him on the other side. Wallace was snoring almost the moment he stretched out. Joel couldn't go to sleep as quickly. The nights seemed to bring memories and thoughts which never plagued him in daylight. Not all of his broodings dealt with Consuela, though she was certainly their dominant theme. She wasn't to blame, for instance, for his growing doubts about this whole campaign. Wouldn't he do better to stifle his feelings and go back to his own knitting?

This was December 23, almost Christmas. They'd been at this monotonous business since the middle of September. For over a month they'd loafed around San Antonio waiting for Sam Houston's general to get ready. Then they'd moped along toward Laredo, leaving the road for some reason only Somervell understood.

Why had Somervell accepted command of the army if he didn't want to fight? Was it all tied up somehow with President Houston's politics? Sam thought so, as did Ben McCulloch. Dick Fisher and Ewen made speeches about Houston's politics at the slightest excuse. Joel grunted and pushed off Big Foot's weight so he could turn over. Politics seemed to be at the bottom of everything men disliked. He wished he'd never heard the word. He wished he was back on the Medina looking after his cattle. Even without Consuela, he wished that. He'd been a fool to go off half-cocked just because she'd left him.

He finally dropped off to sleep only to have Sam arouse him. Walker wanted to turn over and that meant pushing off Acklin and Joel. There was no such thing as sound sleep that cold night.

With daylight the alcalde was willing to meet Fisher's terms. He was sure he could persuade his people to take their boats across the river. He was eager to get away from the Texians and he didn't mind showing it.

"No call for us all going back with him," said McCulloch. "Just that many more boats to worry about."

Sam, Joel, Acklin and Big Foot crossed with the alcalde. On the other side, they hustled the Mexican along until he begged for mercy. *Senors*, his legs were not as long as theirs. Nor his wind as good. Did they want to run him to death? They didn't, just wanted to keep warm. The alcalde was gasping for breath when they finally reached the pueblo.

Joel, helping the pudgy Mexican along, wasn't sure what happened then. All he knew was that suddenly Mexican soldiers swarmed out of the *jacals* and pounced on them. Sam Walker didn't even have a chance to draw his five-shooters. The brown-skinned men had Sam and were after the others before Joel could make a move. He shot one and then heeded Sam's yell to go for it. He whirled and ran for dear life, weaving a little to bother their aim, but not enough to slow him down. The most important thing was to outdistance his pursuers.

He ran as long as he could and then trotted. Looking back, he saw Big Foot floundering along and Acklin not far away. Strung out behind came a stream of screaming pursuers. Joel ducked his head and kept going. The Lord only knew how many Mexican troops had suddenly showed up in Mier. Two hundred, three hundred, a thousand—he couldn't make a good guess. But the terrain between the pueblo and the river was thick with them.

Fifty yards from the stream he heard horsemen and looked back again. Dragoons came bearing down at a dead gallop. Wallace and Acklin had outrun all unmounted pursuit, too. But they'd have a close shave with the lancers. Joel pushed off the skiff and grabbed a paddle. Here came Acklin splashing into the shallow water. Kit plopped into the boat without help. Big Foot got to the river just a jump ahead of the dragoons. He hit the water half-running and half-swimming. Joel plied the paddle, leaving Kit to help the Virginian into the skiff. Bullets were raining around them before Big Foot made it. Wallace fell across the middle seat and lay there gasping while Acklin helped widen the stretch of water between them and the shore. The dragoons had dismounted and were firing futile shots at the bobbing boat.

"Gawdamighty!" groaned Big Foot, getting his breath at last.

Acklin pushed him an oar. "Give us a jump."

The shots had brought most of Fisher's men to the river bank. Taunts and eager questions greeted the trio as they neared the shore. Where had they flushed out the dragoons? How many were there? Where was Walker? Was that Big Foot with them or a whale? Wallace scrambled to shore and shook off water like a spaniel. If they had been in his shoes, he snapped, they wouldn't have thought it so dad-gummed funny. As for Sam—the Mexicans had him.

Mier occupied! McCulloch couldn't believe it. Who had ever heard of Mexicans marching in bad weather? Big Foot must have been seeing things. Them as didn't believe the town swarmed with soldiers, said Big Foot, were danged sure welcome to cross and find out. Joel and Acklin supported his estimate of the enemy's strength. This was no small cavalry detail but a man-sized army. Colonel Fisher's eyes gleamed. He was eager for battle and victory. Nothing short of either would hold his ranks together. And if they were to cut any kind of a caper in Mexico, they needed to get their hands on powder and cannon.

He intended to cross the river immediately. Cameron demurred, and McCulloch. Tom Green was undecided, willing to wait at least until Ben's spies had found out more about the enemy's strength. McCulloch and three others slipped across the river several miles down-stream. They returned near midnight with more positive data about the Mexicans. The quartet had slipped boldly into town and managed to capture a sentry. A bowie slid across the Mexican's throat had induced him to talk. This was General Pedro Ampudia's force of almost two thousand regulars, fully equipped for battle with twenty fieldpieces.

Dick Fisher didn't believe it. Several hundred regulars, he conceded, but not two thousand. Anyhow, the Texians would storm Mier. Green said the same thing. The Texians roused out of their blankets by the commotion generally agreed. Of course the Mexican sentry had stretched the truth. Didn't they always? Ben McCulloch tried to curb their recklessness. Once across the river, he pointed out, they couldn't retreat. And, he felt the sentry had told the truth.

Big Foot said the same thing. "Of course," added the Virginian, "it looks like more of 'em when they're after you."

Cameron proposed a delay of at least forty-eight hours. He was voted down just as he'd been rejected for colonel. These men had tromped for two months looking for Mexicans to fight. Nothing short of a battle would satisfy them.

McCulloch had found out little about Sam Walker. The greaser sentry had claimed to know nothing of any Texian prisoner.

"If they haven't shot him by dawn," Chevaille said grimly, "they've missed their chance. The shoe will be on the other foot by this time tomorrow."

Chapter Thirteen

The Texians moved several miles downstream to make their crossing. Fisher assigned forty men to guard the horses and keep fires blazing. Possibly any Mexican scouts across the stream would be deceived about the enemy camp. They might assure their commanders that the Texians were holed up in their camp and too busy keeping warm to attack.

It was no day for a battle, that was certain. The wind blew hard against their backs as they paddled across the Rio Grande in their borrowed skiffs. McCulloch's "spies" reached the opposite bank first. They spread out thin and held their places. The main force had to be crossed in relays. It was past noon before all had landed, though no man knew that by the sky above him. The sun hadn't broken through yet.

Slowly the Texians moved toward Mier. Colonel Fisher wisely ordered them forward in waves rather than any regular formation. The murky gray light benefited the invaders. Most of them wore homespun or buckskin; with their heads low in their coats, and spread out, they couldn't be seen at any distance. They offered poor targets to any gun batteries.

Ten or twelve paces separated Joel from Big

Foot on one side and Acklin on the other. McCulloch kept ahead, moving restlessly along his line. They advanced slowly, more like men stalking deer than assaulting an enemy town. They caught fleeting glimpses of the pueblo ahead, but the sky never cleared longer than an instant. They were within a mile of Mier when the first cannon sounded. Its shot struck a hundred yards short of the Texians but caused them to quicken their pace. Then they heard approaching horsemen. Tearing through the gloom came a company of dragoons. Ben set the example for his "spies." He took a rifle shot at the enemy riders, then melted off. Joel was sure he hit his target though he didn't wait to see if the lancer fell. He darted after Big Foot. They fanned out in the brush, every man for himself, but all moving toward Mier. Another dragoon detail came seeking them out. Joel squatted in chinnery waist-deep and shot his rifle almost as fast as he could reload. The lancers had small chance of flushing quarries out of this combination of gray overcast and brushy cover. The sure-shooting Texas riflemen coldly exploited their advantage. Every time a dim shape shows on horseback—nail him.

The fog turned into drizzle; there seemed to be no more mounted targets. Joel protected his rifle as best he could with his unbuttoned shirt; he jammed his five-shooters into his pockets. This drizzle promised wet powder and useless guns.

It stilled the Mexican artillery temporarily, a relief to the invaders even if the exploding shells hadn't hurt anyone. An adobe hut suddenly loomed up in front of Joel and he stood under its eaves until Big Foot joined him.

A gun went off near them and lead thudded into the ground a few feet away. Wallace pointed to the next hut.

"Up on the roof," he said. "Let's get 'em."

Joel darted after him. Two other shots challenged them, but they found shelter under the overhanging roof. The *jacal* was some nine feet high. Big Foot tested its height, then told Joel, "Cock your pistol. I'll hoist you up."

Joel nodded. Revolver ready, he rose suddenly over the edge of the flat roof, the big Virginian lifting his weight easily. The three Mexican riflemen were helpless against his quick shots. Joel dropped to the ground and reloaded. He'd fired all five bullets to make sure of his targets.

Gunfire sounded all around them. Joel scrambled up on the next rooftop after killing its two defenders. Big Foot swung up after him and gestured that he meant to catch his breath.

"No call to rush," Wallace said. "This shooting's sure to last a spell."

Musket fire seemed to belch from every *jacal*. In addition the cannon bellowed out again, raking the street from emplacements in the plaza. The grape and cannisters kept the invaders moving from house to house; the pattern of fighting Big Foot and Joel had set went on everywhere. Cavalry charges down the street amounted to nothing. The two hundred Texians did not show themselves except on the rooftops; even then the Mexicans caught only fleeting glimpses of them. Fanned out in two's and three's, the assailants were taking a *jacal* at a time.

Whatever odds were against them were offset by the drizzle and the closely bunched adobe huts. What matter how many regulars Ampudia had arrayed in the plaza? Only a few Mexicans manned any one roof, and these were at a great disadvantage. Their *escopetas* had such recoils that no man could shoulder one for a dead aim. He threw up his musket and fired his single shot while his cool adversary took aim, then countered with unerring marksmanship. The Texians with five-shooters were particularly invincible in such close-quarter combat. Big Foot and Joel, rising up on a roof, had twenty bullets each—four or five times what they faced.

The attached houses near the center of town were harder to take. The Mexicans abandoned the rooftops to shoot from behind the cover of thick walls. The invader who let himself be seen atop one of the structures took his life in his hands. The Texians resorted to breaking through partition walls. Using captured crowbars, picks and their own bowies, they dug and smashed their way forward. Acklin, Chevaille and Buck Barry joined Big Foot and Joel. Three dug and pounded while the other two covered the breach with their pistols. Picks thudded out loopholes so they could fire at the Mexican dragoons in the street.

No detail knew how the battle went elsewhere. Joel's bunch seized a hut, held it, hammered out an opening to the next. It grew to be monotonous business, especially as the enemy usually fled into the street before the Texians could open fire. Once or twice they stopped to rest and to wonder what was happening outside. Acklin ventured up on a roof and returned with the discouraging report that they were still a half-mile from the plaza. The drizzle hadn't let up and the gloom seemed to be thickening.

The next *jacal* yielded food. Apparently a large-sized family had set out its meal before fleeing. There were *chili con carne*, *tortillas* and *pulque* left after the quintet had eaten their fill. Big Foot slipped outside and invited another detail to finish up. McCulloch and his followers gratefully cleaned the table.

No man was in a hurry to attack the next wall. Joel stretched out on the floor and listened to Big Foot argue the advantages of a heavy-butted rifle. This was eerie business, Joel thought. Their adobe shelter tempered the battle sounds. From inside the hut the shooting seemed to be a long way off. But McCulloch said the fighting was getting harder every minute. Joe Berry was down with a bullet in his thigh. Ben had dragged the wounded ranger to a *jacal* where Dr. J. J. Sinnickson was treating the wounded. The Doc had come along as a fighting man but now he was plying his trade. John E. Jones, an Englishman who had ridden with the rangers since spring, was dead. How were the other companies doing? McCulloch had seen enough of the battle to predict what came next. By noon the next day they'd be closing in on the plaza. No telling what would happen if the Mexicans made a life or death stand there. Could the Texians whip the Mexicans in an open battle? Ben voiced his doubts.

"Not without horses," he said. He hadn't liked invading Mexico afoot. He claimed that their superior horsemanship usually proved their ace in the hole.

"Well," said Big Foot, picking up his crowbar, "this ain't whipping nobody. Come on, you galoots. We may never take this town but we'll danged sure wreck it."

McCulloch darted back into the street, braving the artillery bursts to reach Colonel Fisher's temporary headquarters. He met pessimism there. One company, said Fisher, was already low on powder. At least fifty Texians couldn't fire their rifles. Some had fallen into filled *acequias*; others hadn't protected their guns from the drizzle. McCulloch reported his "spies" moving up steadily. Had anybody heard from Ewen Cameron? The man who asked the question was sent to find the Scot. Back into the open went McCulloch. Cameron's company was supposed to be attacking the town from the east. The cowboy brigade was taking one hut at a time like the rangers. Cameron reported some losses but nothing like the doleful toll taken of Fisher's and Eastland's groups. Were his men running low on powder?

"Aye," said Ewen. "But when we're out of powder, we'll cut them down with our knives. Tell Fisher not to worry about us. We'll get to the plaza afore him."

His Scotch accent was stronger than ever.

McCulloch transmitted this information to Fisher and rejoined his own men. Dark had fallen, but the flashes of cannon guided him along. He found Pipgras and Davis holed up for the night with Big Foot's quartet. Bill Barkley was dead. A handful of Mexicans had refused to flee one of the *jacals* while they had the chance. Barkley, first man through the breached wall, had been killed at once. All six of the enemy were dead, too, if that was any consolation.

Outside, the Mexican cavalry tore up and down the streets. Cannon boomed out regularly. Once a heavy shot thundered into the roof above Joel and a segment of it collapsed. But that was the only threat to their safety that night. They had no idea of what the enemy lancers were accomplishing with their sallies, or even what they were sup-posed to be doing.

Joel could have slept except for the noise. Two men were enough to guard their own breach. He did stretch out and close his eyes, and once or twice he dozed off. Here in the heart of a furious battle they rested snug and cozy.

But, moving on with daylight, they found the fighting still fierce. They burst into the last of the attached *jacals*. They peered out through jagged loopholes at the plaza with its artillery. The range was too great for any gun but Big Foot's. He thrust "Sweet Lips" through an opening and squinted down its barrel. His satisfied grunt announced that he had hit his target.

Nothing would do McCulloch but to venture up on the roof. Down he scrambled a few moments later. He could estimate the positions of the other Texians. Ewen Cameron's deadly house wreckers were within two hundred yards of the plaza. Eastland's company was farther back; Fisher's group had advanced a little closer since the night before. They'd better be getting worried, said Ben. He saw nothing to prevent the Mexicans from isolating the various units and subduing them one by one. They'd better get up on the roof, he said, where they could do some good.

Joel wriggled to the edge and peered down cautiously. A group of horsemen came galloping along; he, Acklin, Pipgras and Davis blazed away. The restless McCulloch dashed off to find Fisher. Big Foot abandoned his loophole in favor of the roof. Sure, he was safer behind the walls but he wanted company. Mexican sharpshooters across the street trained *escopetas* on their housetop. Joel and his companions lay flat on their stomachs while the bullets screamed overhead. Big Foot looked up to see lancers bearing down on them.

"Look out," he yelled, and dropped a dragoon with "Sweet Lips." The cavalrymen dismounted and sought shelter under the overhanging eaves. In a few moments they tried to clamber up, a score or more of them. Evidently they were ordered to take the roof at any cost. The three rangers with repeating pistols lay prone and shot down the reckless dragoons as they reached the edge of the roof. Big Foot called cadence so that two sets of revolvers were in action while the third man reloaded his smoking guns.

Minutes passed and still McCulloch did not return. Somebody yelled from across the street. Mike Chevaille was braving enemy bullets to voice his greeting. Joel rose up for a quick look. Chevaille had eight or nine companions; Joel couldn't be sure. They huddled together under furious *escopeta* fire and wondered if these were all the survivors of the "spy" company. If so, they'd lost half of their number gaining the plaza.

McCulloch finally rejoined them. His shoulder was bleeding, but he insisted it was only a scratch. It was rough back there, he said grimly. The Mexicans had overpowered the makeshift hospital and captured Dr. Sinnickson along with the wounded men. Eastland's company didn't have enough powder to hold off a mass attack. Fisher had ordered the Texians to fight their way back together. Two hundred yards or so behind them, and to their right, was an open courtyard with a high stone wall, roomy enough for a united stand. Ewen Cameron's company held it now. The courtyard, in fact, had halted the Scot's advance.

They lost Davis crossing to the next housetop —hit in the leg. There was no carrying him along. Big Foot left Tom his water gourd and they leaped to the next roof. They glimpsed Chevaille's bunch heading in the same direction.

Dragoons still ranged the street, firing up at every movement on the roofs. Grape and cannister raked the housetops, too. A ball thudded just ahead of Joel and sent him sprawling backward. He would have fallen without Kit Acklin's helping hand.

They leaped to the ground and darted to the courtyard walls. Up scrambled Joel after a boost from Big Foot. Then he and Acklin helped pull Wallace over the wall. Ewen Cameron assisted the Virginian to his feet after Big Foot had sprawled inside.

"Steady," said the Scot. His eyes met Joel's and Ewen held out his hand in a quick gesture. "Glad you're here, lad," he said. "We have work to do."

He gestured for them to help his men pile up stones under the thick walls. The rangers fell too quickly. No use to ask what the stones were for. Ewen meant to save powder as much as possible. Don't shoot a Mexican if his skull can be bashed in.

The stone wall was about six feet high; the taller men could stand on the rock piles and see what was going on outside. The enemy artillery had shifted its sights to concentrate on the court-yard. Every minute a shell screamed into the enclosure. Across the street a company of Texians formed to make a rush for the stone barricade. Joel saw Colonel Fisher, hatless, clothing torn, and Bill Eastland, limping as if hit. Dragoons galloped down to intercept them. Joel, Big Foot and a dozen others vaulted up on the wall to empty their pistols at the cavalrymen. Fisher stumbled and fell. Two companions pulled him up and brought him to the wall. Wallace and Joel caught hold of the commander's arms and pulled him to safety. The hottest fighting in Joel's experience ended with the sudden retreat of the lancers. At least twenty bodies in glittering uniforms were left sprawled behind them.

The rumor started that Colonel Fisher was

killed, but his wound proved to be nothing more serious than the loss of his right thumb. A Mexican bullet had snipped it neatly. But Fisher seemed to be suffering greatly. His head was lolling forward as he sat on the ground, he was pale and haggard and he vomited several times.

Ben McCulloch stationed his rangers along the south wall without waiting for orders. Ewen took the north parapet. Joel looked up and down the uneven line of rangers. He counted twenty-six, including himself. So only six or seven were missing. McCulloch declined to be elated about this.

"We've done all right this far, but the worst is yet to come."

An assault on the north wall claimed their full attention. Some Mexican officer must have lost his senses, for a force of less than fifty infantry-men tried to scale the parapet. Ewen scorned help, though nearly every Texian in the court-yard took shots at the men. The Mexicans who managed to clear the wall were knifed or battered with stones.

No other assault came for a while, but Ampudia's guns hurled shot after shot into the enclosure. It was wasted effort; the Texians crouched against the walls and jeered the efforts to subdue them with grape and cannister. Then the bombardment suddenly stopped. For the first time since daylight the fighting lulled.

Joel watched curiously as the Texian captains gathered around Colonel Fisher. Nobody else considered the commander's wound serious, but he seemed to believe he was at death's door. If he cared two hoots about what his captains were saying, he didn't show it.

Tom Green seemed to be talking the most. Ewen didn't appreciate his ideas; the Scot kept shaking his head. Bill Eastland seemed to agree with Green.

"What's there to jaw about?" demanded Chevaille. "We ain't going nowhere and there ain't but one thing to do—shoot every one of the devils we can."

"It ain't that simple," said Acklin. "Your trouble is that you don't think like an officer. There's got to be speeches. Wars don't amount to much without 'em."

"Reckon that's what I like most about Jack," said Mike. "He's no hand for palaver."

A bugle sounded, clear and close at hand. Several Texians scrambled up on the walls to see what was happening. Their excited versions brought others atop the parapet. The street was cleared of all Mexican troops except the bugler. By him stood Dr. Sinnickson, waiting for recognition from the courtyard. Tom Green shouted out a question. He seemed to have taken charge without an election or even a formal announcement that Fisher was surrendering command.

The doctor brought terms from General Pedro Ampudia. Did the Texians want to hear them?

The first reaction was both vigorous and profane. They weren't about to talk terms. But Colonel Fisher rose up from the ground. Apparently he had decided that he would live despite his missing thumb. He'd hear the terms, he announced. Dr. Sinnickson came to the foot of the wall. He had Ampudia's offer in writing. The Texians were hopelessly trapped, declared the Mexican commander. He had two thousand regular troops and expected reinforcements from Monterey. Without food or water the invaders could not hold the courtyard long. He was anxious to avoid further loss of life. Let the Texians lay down their arms and Ampudia would treat them with humanity and deference as prisoners of war. He would use his influence to retain them as prisoners along the border until they were released or exchanged.

Fisher sent the physician back with word that he would hold a council of his captains immediately. The Texians would respect a truce until they had reached a decision.

Fisher, Green, Eastland, McCulloch, Cameron —these five began deliberation. Others joined them. Of a sudden there were more "captains" than the men in the ranks had realized. And somebody swung open the courtyard gate to admit several Mexican officers and a padre.

These officers greeted Fisher with warm smiles and embraces.

"Just what's going on?" growled Big Foot.

Joel shook his head. He certainly didn't know. The meeting of captains was breaking up in furious argument. Tom Green and Ewen Cameron looked fit to be tied. Neither wanted to surrender, nor did McCulloch. Green's voice rose above the others. He wasn't about to trust any Mexican offer of terms. Cameron vowed that his company would fight on regardless of what the others did. Finally Fisher went off with the priest, officers and Dr. Sinnickson to personally confirm General Ampudia's intentions.

Fisher returned shortly and called for a general meeting. He had known Ampudia for years, he said. The Mexican commander was an honorable man. Those who surrendered could be sure of honorable treatment. The odds were stacked against them in this courtyard. They had neither food nor water and their powder was almost gone. Their only hope was to break out and risk their lives in a desperate dash for the river. A few survivors might fight their way back to Texas but only a few. Ampudia had not exaggerated his strength; they were outnumbered ten to one. This could be another Alamo if the Texians insisted, for Ampudia meant to raise the black flag if his terms were refused. Their captains had not been able to reach an agreement, so he was referring the decision to the men themselves. Let those who wished to, march out of the courtyard and lay down their arms.

Some began moving immediately—men of Eastland's company, of Tom Green's, despite their captain's militant stand. Joel looked uneasily at Big Foot, then Acklin. They were waiting for a clue from McCulloch.

"Shucks, I don't know what to tell you," Ben said disgustedly. "Reckon it has to be every man for himself."

With that, one of the rangers started for the gate. Joel licked his lips and decided to wait for a sign from Wallace. Slowly other Texians moved toward the gate. Nobody wanted to jeer at them as cowards or even call them back. Colonel Fisher had not exaggerated the odds against them. Joel stood waiting with less than two dozen shots left for his revolvers and only eight or nine charges of powder for his rifle. Half of the Texians carried useless guns now, good only for clubbing. With a sinking heart Joel realized that the decision was already made; some Texians were just more reluctant to admit it than others. Even McCulloch, Cameron and Green saw the handwriting on the wall. A hundred men left in the courtyard now—then eighty—sixty!

"Well," grunted Big Foot, "we might as well get it over with."

Joel sighed and followed after Wallace.

Chapter Fourteen

Eager brown hands clutched at the rifles, pistols and knives the Texians reluctantly gave up. Joel was among the last, holding on to his five-shooters as long as possible. But finally they were all disarmed and formed into irregular ranks. An overjoyed Mexican colonel started them marching across the plaza to the stone presidio. Other Mexican soldiers scurried ahead to open heavy iron-studded doors. The presidio's courtyard was small; fifty men would have been crowded in it. Four times that many were herded through the gates. Bayonets, lances and swords threatened those who demurred.

Somebody came pushing through the mass of Texians: Sam Walker. He was no worse for his imprisonment, except that he hadn't been fed. He'd followed the battle as best he could from his cell.

"What did you quit for?" he demanded. "You were whipping the daylights out of 'em!"

Nobody could tell him. Already they could see what was ahead of them.

Captain Manuel Canales took no part in the riotous celebration as the presidio gates shut after the Texians. He wanted to. He would have liked nothing better than to forget his dignity and rank and join the exultant soldiers stripping the dead invaders and dragging their bodies through the streets. Especially was Canales delighted to learn that the captives included Ewen Cameron's cowboys.

Manuel had hoped so—and hoped against hope that a certain copper-haired gringo was still numbered among Cameron's following. He could imagine nothing sweeter than to gloat over Joel Howard's misery, especially if he wangled the assignment as commander of their guards. The Texians had no sooner surrendered than Manuel asked his uncle to use his influence with Ampudia.

Captain Canales' request was quickly granted. There were no bigger heroes of Mier than the Canales, uncle and nephew. Manuel fairly oozed his delight as he took over his new responsibility —to march the Texians to Salado under irons and confine them there until Santa Anna's orders were clarified.

There was quite a conference about those orders—to which Manuel was not admitted. But he knew their gist and he was as pleased about that as his uncle. General Ampudia was not, however, and Governor Mexia was reportedly defiant. But neither, mused Manuel, were apt to dispute Santa Anna's authority.

The Texians were packed in the courtyard so

tightly that there was no stirring around. Manuel mounted the stone wall and gloated over their compact mass. Here, he thought, was the ideal place for execution. Mexican soldiers could shoot leisurely from the presidio walls until every Texian was killed. There would be no escaping men as at Goliad, when the intended victims had been marched out onto an open plain not very far from a river. But Santa Anna's orders called for these unkempt scoundrels to be marched forty-odd miles, and so it would be. Manuel Canales would supervise that march with loving care. The Texian who broke ranks, as if to get away, would not take more than a few steps.

Though his own English was more than adequate, Captain Canales had selected Dr. Sinnickson to interpret. The physician tried to beg off. His fellow countrymen, he explained sadly, were already bitter against him for his role in arranging the surrender. Almost to a man, now, the Texians were convinced that their capitulation had been a grievous mistake. Couldn't Canales choose another prisoner?

Manuel's lip curled. He had given an order, he snapped. Let the good doctor obey or face the consequences. The sooner the Texian dogs learned that his orders would be obeyed to the letter, the better for them. Dr. Sinnickson yielded and stood by the captain's side on the stone wall.

There was no doubting this captain's capabilities for cruelty. Dr. Sinnickson translated Canales' words into English. The prisoners would be marched to Salado the next morning. In the meantime they were to line up by two's to receive their fetters.

Angry protests drowned out the doctor's words. They had surrendered as prisoners of war! Where was Ampudia? He had personally guaranteed them honorable treatment. Dick Fisher was shoved forward as their spokesman. Canales looked down coldly from atop the wall and refused permission for Fisher to come up beside him. Let the Texian talk from the ground. But he might as well save his breath.

"It's just like I told you," Chevaille growled. Joel nodded. His own hopes had died the instant he recognized Manuel Canales.

"You talked us into this," roared Green at Fisher. "Now talk us out of it."

In any other circumstances Joel would have pitied Fisher. Desperately, Dick tried to explain that he had been duped. He would have sworn that they could trust Ampudia's word anywhere and anytime. Manuel listened to the harangue with a cold smile. It was pleasant to watch the Texians squirm and berate their elected leader. Finally Manuel spoke to Dr. Sinnickson and the physician quieted the tumult long enough to be heard.

He repeated the truth—that any terms General Ampudia might have spoken about, meant nothing. The orders for disposition of the prisoners had come direct from Santa Anna.

Another demonstration. Canales allowed it. It amused him to watch these gringos brandish their fists. He smiled at their coarse, profane threats. Listening to them, one could almost believe that they did menace El Presidente's safety as well as Mexico's existence. Would they still voice such defiance after they had struggled to Salado with their heavy manacles? He would find out.

Canales motioned for more soldiers to join him on the wall. These crouched, holding their *escopetas* ready. The unhappy physician repeated Manuel's threat. If the Texians had not paired off in sixty seconds, he would order the garrison to start firing.

Dick Fisher stood speechless, helpless. So did Tom Green. In that moment of indecision, Ewen Cameron proved his qualities of leadership.

"Listen to me," he roared out. "You men know I argued against surrender. I was the last captain to give in. But we've done it and now we can do nothing but make the best of it. Don't doubt for a moment that those devils won't shoot us down in this very courtyard." He looked up at Canales. "Where do we line up?" he demanded.

Canales gestured toward a door opening into a small storeroom. There a half-dozen blacksmiths were waiting with their anvils and glowing fires.

Cameron stepped forward to be the first in line. Tom Green moved quickly to take the place beside him.

"Wal," Sam Walker said loudly, "it took Ewen to show us what to do. Come on, young 'un."

Joel shook his head. He had no intention of resisting but he dreaded to face Manuel Canales. Perhaps if he hung back he could be spared that ordeal.

Sam grunted at Joel's explanation. "Lordee," he said, "you're in for it. If that Canales has his way, you'll get skinned alive."

Slowly, but not silently, the other Texians followed the example of Cameron, Green and Walker. Fisher would have liked to be among the last, but his resentful countrymen jostled him forward. Joel let the others push by him.

Canales had hurried down from the wall to personally supervise the work of his blacksmiths. His eyes glowed as Cameron entered the make-shift smithy, stooping to get through the low door. That was good, thought Canales. He had long wanted to see this tall Scot bow his head before Mexican authority.

"*Buenas dias*, Captain Cameron," taunted Manuel. "I had hoped to find you among my prisoners."

"It was not my choice," snapped Ewen even as he allowed the chain to be pulled around his leg. "I would have fought you to the death and you know it. So does your uncle."

"We do, indeed," Canales said with a shrug. "And it may well be that you have."

The Scot straightened up. "What do you mean by that?"

Manuel scowled and declined to answer. Instead, he ordered the blacksmiths to hurry. "You can't take all day with one prisoner," he snapped at his underlings. "I want every last one of them in manacles by sundown."

"*Si,*" muttered the smiths, wielding their hammers at a faster pace. They had good reason to tremble when Captain Canales was displeased.

Two by two came the other prisoners. Occasionally Canales demanded their names. The reputa-tions of Sam Walker, Ben McCulloch and Big Foot Wallace had spread south of the Rio Grande. Jack Hays was missing, and Manuel deplored that. So did Ampudia and his uncle. Santa Anna's dispatches had cited the ranger leader. If among the invaders, Hays should be killed or taken at all costs. No Texians had done more to injurc Mexican pride than these hard-riding men with their diabolical revolvers.

Canales finally wearied of his grim sport. He turned and started to leave, then decided to step out into the courtyard and look over the remaining prisoners. His eyes fell upon the tall figure of Joel Howard and he fairly chortled. Bless not only his patron saint but all others! There stood the gringo he wanted most to see. And this *Senor* Howard wished very much to avoid his recognition; that was as obvious as the color of the gringo's hair.

"Ah, *Senor* Howard," Manuel said softly. "This is indeed a great moment."

Joel had lost his hat somewhere in the fighting. He pushed back his unruly hair and faced Canales defiantly.

"A great moment," repeated Manuel. "Before you receive your irons, *senor*, I will tell you about the *Senorita* O'Rourke. She has returned to her grandfather's hacienda. She is awaiting the end of this sorry business. I have been promised her hand as soon as I can be spared from my duties here."

"Not while I live," Joel blurted out.

The sergeant in charge of the blacksmiths indicated they were ready for Joel.

"Step forward and get your irons, *senor*," taunted Canales. "I'm sure they will be most becoming to you."

Chapter Fifteen

They marched out of Mier in double file, Canales riding ahead on his black horse. Two hundred dragoons went along as guards, more than one to every prisoner; they rode in double ranks encircling the Texians. Whenever their vigilance relaxed, Captain Canales doubled back with his invectives and threats. It took only a short time for other Texians to share Joel's personal hatred for the captain. The men afoot must keep pace with the dragoons. True, the lancers rode their horses at a walk, but even so it was a killing gait. A man did not ordinarily walk as fast as a horse, especially not when heavily fettered. Joel, striding along with Sam, was not indifferent to Canales' personal attention. Let him lag, Joel knew, and the captain would demonstrate he had meant his orders.

Consuela had reached Agua Dulce safely! The relief of that was almost worth the accompanying announcement—that she was betrothed to Canales. Joel struggled against believing that. His only authority for the statement was Canales himself, and once before Manuel had lied. The Spaniard had stood outside the Garza hacienda and declared himself Consuela's affianced. But he hadn't been then, and he might not be now. At least, thought Joel, he would cling to that hope as long as he could.

The cold wave still held; the Texians shivered as they plodded on. But their suffering had just begun; night caught them still ten or twelve miles from Salado. They would have preferred to march on in the dark but their Mexican captors were concerned about their own comfort. They had blankets as well as thick serapes; they could sleep that night. Let the Texian dogs huddle against each other for warmth.

Canales allowed a large fire, requiring the prisoners to lie in a circle around it. His dragoons enjoyed their own blazes, dozens of them. The watch was divided equally among the lancers. At no time were less than fifty Mexicans watching the uncomfortable prisoners.

The Texians had paired off as they pleased, and Joel was curled up with Sam, Chevaille, Wallace, McCulloch, Acklin. They pressed Joel for an explanation of Canales' hostility. He told them most of it, including the ambush he had survived.

"Did he threaten you?" Walker wanted to know.

"Sure."

"He did Ewen, too. Hinted that Ewen might just as well have fought on to the death."

"Ain't no use to hoorah about it," Acklin said bitterly. "They aim to kill us. Did from the start."

173

"I don't figger that," said McCulloch. "I'll take what the captain said. Ampudia doesn't have the say about what's done with us. We can thank Santa Anna himself for what happens."

"Then why are they marching us to Salado?" demanded Mike. "Why didn't they just shoot us back there?"

Ben shook his head. He didn't know. But the Mexicans had done almost the same thing at Goliad; had marched the Texians a long way for a brief confinement before ordering them out to be shot. Acklin sighed as he shifted the weight of his iron ball to the other hand.

"And there ain't a chance of getting away," he brooded.

Nobody argued. Mike was right. Captain Manuel Canales was no ordinary jailer.

The prisoners had a skimpy supper—cold corncakes and ground meat that was mostly gristle. Breakfast was the same.

"They danged sure don't believe in fattening a man for the kill," grumbled Acklin.

Canales had them moving again shortly after sunrise. The first incident occurred before they had gone a mile. A ranger, Bill Thompson, suddenly sat down and balked at taking another step. Blood was oozing from a bullet wound in his thigh. Somehow he'd managed to keep up the day before but he refused to try it another day.

"Get up, Bill," argued Sam, "they'll shoot you like a dog."

"Let 'em," said Thompson. "Let 'em shoot, damn their dirty souls."

Three dragoons dismounted and threatened the sitting man with their gun butts. Thompson didn't stir. He had torn his trousers so that his wound showed. He pointed to it and shrugged his shoulders. He couldn't rattle off Spanish in reply to their excited threats, but he made his meaning clear.

Canales galloped back on his black horse to see what was holding up the line. Joel guessed that the captain asked if the dragoons had threatened to shoot Thompson. Answered in the affirmative, Canales scowled. But he didn't order the dragoons to use either their lances or *escopetas*. Instead, he rattled off orders and another dragoon dismounted. To the surprise of every watching Texian, the disgruntled lancer took Thompson up behind him. And they rode double until the inhabitants of the next pueblo produced a donkey for the prisoner.

His fellow Texians grinned every time they looked back at the lanky Thompson. He cut a sorry figure on the small, shaggy burro, but they had to admire his cool determination. His demonstration gave them a lift. Bill Thompson surely hadn't been afraid of death. He'd looked up at the menacing Mexicans and spoken his piece without flinching. And Canales had done the backing down.

When Canales called a halt to water their horses, several dragoons even showed solicitude for Thompson. *Pobrecito cojo*, they called him— poor lame boy. One of the lancers took off his sash for Bill to use as a bandage. Another brought him water in a gourd. When they walked off, Thompson's eyes held a twinkle. He whispered to McCulloch that he wasn't hurt too badly. He had just made up his mind not to do any more walking.

On they marched until Salado appeared before them. The adobe houses and stone presidio meant the end of their torturous march, but no prisoner was elated over it. For the town's entire population, it seemed, turned out to celebrate the capture of the dreaded Texians. Firecrackers popped, cracked church bells clanged, children ran about excitedly with banners. Twice, three times, the enchained men were paraded around the central plaza. Only then were they herded into three cells large enough for two dozen prisoners, but certainly unbearable for two hundred.

Next afternoon they were ordered to form ranks in the courtyard. Something was up. Mexican soldiers completely encircled them, and as many more watched from the stone walls. Whispers flew thick and fast. Suspense mounted as a Colonel Domingo Huerta mounted a parapet and demanded their close attention.

He immediately dashed any hopes about their prospects of release. He ordered the prisoners handcuffed by pairs, and his soldiers hurried to carry out his command. Joel stood next to Sam but wasn't paired off so. He was manacled to Big Foot, and Walker was fastened to Chevaille.

Then Colonel Huerta read off the contents of an impressive-looking paper—Santa Anna's final orders. Dr. Sinnickson slowly and tonelessly interpreted the high-sounding phrases. Without his simplification of the words, most of the Texians wouldn't have understood the decree. Santa Anna, in the name of the Supreme Government of Mexico, declared the Texians to be brigands and decreed the execution of every tenth man.

Colonel Huerta finished reading the document, then explained how the executions would be managed. Seventeen men would be shot, he said. They would be chosen by lot. A lieutenant brought forward a jar shaped like a gourd and covered with a dark cloth. Another produced a small table. Carefully the colonel counted out one hundred and fifty-nine white beans and seventeen black ones. He poured these into the jar and shook it thoroughly.

Meanwhile, Dr. Sinnickson repeated Huerta's explanations. Every man drawing a black bean would be shot immediately. First the Texian officers would draw, then the men, in alphabetical order. There would be no swapping of beans.

177

If a Texian withdrew more than one bean, and one was black, he would be one of the seventeen executed.

The first name was called.

"Captain Ewen Cameron."

The Texians had heard the manifesto through without demonstration. Without moving, in fact. Death for seventeen men by lottery! Joel's first thought was to wonder if either Mexia or Ampudia had approved of such a cold-blooded deal.

"Captain Ewen Cameron!"

Joel craned his neck. Ewen stood in line twenty paces from him. The Scot hadn't moved.

"Goddammit!" somebody cried hoarsely. "Let's rush 'em."

Not a man stirred, not even to echo this defiance. What chance did they have, handcuffed together, against such armed numbers? This could be a trick of some sort intended to goad them into violence. All eyes watched Ewen Cameron. Joel saw the Scot's jaw muscles twitch. Then Ewen stepped forward with Bill Wilson and dipped his hand beneath the dark cloth. Wilson announced the results.

"White!"

A faint hoarse sound swept along the line of Texians, each man voicing reaction in his own way. Cameron started to step back but Wilson appealed to Colonel Huerta.

"Lemme draw now," he urged. "No call to drag Ewen back up here."

Huerta's frown showed that he understood the request. The colonel conferred with one of his aides, then modified his order. From now on the Texians would draw in pairs. Why not? Seventeen black beans had to be drawn. And why be so squeamish about officers drawing before enlisted men? Rank was immaterial to these Texians at any time, especially now.

McCulloch and Acklin—white beans both. Reprieves for the next handcuffed pair, too. Captain William F. Eastland took out the first black bean. He held it between thumb and forefinger a moment, then raised it for all to see.

"Reckon that's justice," he said slowly. "Nobody wanted this scrap any more than me."

The example was set; from then on a man stepped up quickly as his name was called, and showed no emotion if the draw went against him. "Just my luck," grumbled the next unfortunate. Mike Chevaille's name was called early, of course. Mike's bean was white. He studied it a moment, then flipped it toward Colonel Huerta. The Mexican officer's face flickered as the bean rolled across the ground for his aide to retrieve, but he didn't reprimand Mike for the gesture.

Now Walker's draw. Joel looked off. What irony if Sam should join Eastland and the other unfortunates against the wall! In a hundred-odd skirmishes with Indians and Mexicans he'd never received a serious wound. He'd known no closer brush with death than his bout with the ladino on the lower Medina. If Walker wasn't indestructible, then who was?

Joel couldn't help looking, after all. Sam's hand disappeared under the cloth. He seemed to be making his selection carefully. Up came his closed fist, and opened—with as white a bean as any man had drawn yet.

Sam and Mike rejoined the line. Joel sensed that Walker wanted to tell him something, and edged closer.

"Feel around," whispered Sam. "The black beans are a mite smaller. And harder."

Joel nodded. Somehow the tip didn't surprise him. Trust Sam to be cool, to figure out a way to lower the odds of death.

One of the next pair drew black. He managed to joke about it. Joel knew him only as Ed. "You wuz griping about the cold last night," Ed told his companion. "Well, you got an extra blanket now." The companion had no answer. Another twosome took their place, with the same luck: one black, one white.

"Joel Howard!"

Joel started. His eyes swept the rows of Mexicans on the walls, for his first thought was of Manuel Canales. The captain would relish this. But if Canales was there, Joel didn't see him.

"Me and you, young 'un," Big Foot said gruffly. "You first."

Joel thrust his hand into the jar, running several beans through his fingers. Was there really a difference in their size and firmness? He couldn't be sure, but he thought so. Discarding the others, he pulled out his choice. It was white, all right, oyster white. He struggled to equal the calmness of Walker and Chevaille. It wasn't easy to do. He closed his eyes a second, then watched Big Foot. Either Wallace had overheard Walker's whisper or had reached the same conclusions himself, for he was deliberate about his selection, too. And his bean was as white as Joel's.

Huerta's aide reached out for the black beans as they were drawn and little time was lost in separating the condemned men. There was no fuss about it, no noise except for the clicking of steel. Five Texians still hadn't drawn when the aide announced that all the crucial beans were drawn. Colonel Huerta promptly stopped the lottery.

The Mexican commander snapped orders and the seventeen luckless men were hustled out of sight. The survivors were herded back to confinement. The heavy doors had no sooner closed behind them than they heard the rattle of musketry. A second volley sounded almost as quickly.

"Goddamit!" cursed McCulloch as the third volley roared out. "Can't they even hit standing targets!"

181

Finally the shooting stopped. But shortly Colonel Huerta came. Santa Anna's decree had specified that Captain Ewen Cameron be executed regardless of what he drew. Governor Mexia had withheld enforcement of the order for a very humane reason. He had hoped that the Scot might pluck out one of the deadly beans. When he didn't, Mexia sent Huerta to carry out El Presidente's command. Ewen was in another cell; Joel couldn't see how he took the verdict. He only saw Ewen walking along the corridor, a stride ahead of his guards. He didn't waver, thought Joel, staring after him. Tears welled in Joel's eyes. Santa Anna had been smart to single out Ewen. The Scot would never relent in his fierce hostility toward all things Mexican. If it was an unreasonable prejudice, then Cameron was ready to die for it.

Joel shuddered and waited for the tell-tale volley. He thought he heard it, but wasn't sure. He listened closer, straining his ears. No other sound came. Apparently Huerta's firing squad improved with practice.

Joel shook his head. Ewen had shaken hands with him in the heat of the fight for Mier—how good it was to remember that.

The same Huerta reentered the presidio to announce that the survivors would be marched to Mexico City, and forced to labor on public roads.

Chapter Sixteen

This time the prisoners were manacled by their wrists. In pairs, they trudged out of Salado after a grisly experience none would ever forget. By direct orders of Santa Anna they were forced to parade past the corpses of their eighteen companions, and to look upon the ditch in which the black bean victims would be buried.

Another officer commanded their hundred-odd guards, Colonel Ricardo Vega. He was every bit as callous as his predecessor, but the change elated Joel. At least this wasn't Manuel Canales. The sight of Colonel Vega didn't rouse bitter recollections and start miserable apprehensions about the future. Joel quickly formed a hatred for the squat Mexican and his bristly mustache, yes. How else could he feel about a man who shrugged his shoulders and strode off when Joel and Big Foot showed their manacles cramped their flesh—who halted marches early so his privates could pitch his tent and set up a table for his dinner—who smiled broadly as he paraded his charges through pueblos for townspeople to jeer and even spit upon?

Only one prisoner received Vega's consideration, the same Bill Thompson. Another donkey was provided Thompson after the same cool refusal to walk on his injured leg. Every Texian, by now, knew Bill was shamming and marveled how his act could fool anyone. Big Foot got no relief at all from the Mexican officers and his was very obvious suffering. These manacles might fit the average man, but not big-framed men like Wallace and Joel. The irons cut into Big Foot's wrists so that his flesh turned purple and swelled, bringing even more pain.

But on they trooped with no attention paid to their complaints. Every pueblo was the scene of a triumphant demonstration. Placards posted in the plazas advertised the coming of the captured gringos. Weary, half-starved, dispirited, they finally trudged into San Luis Potosi, expecting the same reception on a bigger scale.

But they didn't get it. The governor of the province came to the plaza to make their entrance an official sort of function, and brought his wife and other fashionably dressed ladies along. Instead of reviling the ragged derelicts, these ladies voiced shock and indignation. The governor quickly echoed their sentiments. The manacles were removed on the spot, and the governor's lady herself treated Big Foot's swollen wrists. Colonel Vega marched them on, with ultimatums about their future treatment ringing in his ears.

The governor's lady—would they ever forget her! From that day on the Texians were different men. Shorter marches, better rations, less personal abuse—even their arrival at grim Perote Prison didn't plunge them back into dejection.

And the announcement that they would be put to work on a road for Santa Anna's personal use brought crooked grins to their grizzled faces. Eyes gleamed with more than amusement as they heard their orders. On weekdays they would work out of nearby Molina del Ray prison, being returned to Perote for the weekends. Let the prisoners work diligently, promised their new commandant, and there would be no trouble.

"Oh, sure," muttered Sam. "Just leave it to us. We'll build old Santa Anna the fanciest road on this continent."

A week later, Joel, Big Foot and Sam were hitched to small carts and told to pull loads of dirt for the road builders.

Captain Pedro Gomez explained the action as soldiers buckled on the harnesses. He deplored the necessity of treating the Texians like donkeys, but what else could he do? Almost tearfully he recited the circumstances requiring such an indignity. He was a well-meaning man with every intention of treating the prisoners decently. He fed them as well as their modest allowances permitted. It wasn't his idea to work the Texians on the road; Santa Anna himself had ordered it. All he, Gomez, required of the captives was a reasonable amount of work. And what did the Texians do? They slacked off and tormented him at every turn. Had *Senors* Wallace, Howard and Walker carried sacks of sand and gravel on their shoulders as directed? No. They'd ripped holes in the sacks so that the sand and gravel spilled out before the road-bed was reached. At the rate they were going the road wouldn't be finished in a hundred years. Did the Texians want him stood against a wall and shot! Any day Santa Anna might lose his temper about the continued necessity to detour between his summer palace and the pueblo of Molino del Ray.

Now, said the exasperated captain, his three biggest troublemakers were harnessed to carts. He hoped they would pull their loads obediently. But if they didn't—the pudgy captain waved his hands helplessly. A drover was assigned to each of the Texians, a drover with a long bullwhip. Balky donkeys sometimes had to be lashed into action. Captain Gomez hoped it wouldn't be necessary to use whips on the prisoners.

Walker grinned and spat tobacco juice out of the corner of his mouth.

"Well, young 'un," he said cheerfully, "we asked for it."

"Sure did," Joel ruefully agreed. He strained forward, testing the weight of his wagon and load. He could pull it all right, but not easily.

The other Texians had already been put to work, with pickaxes or tampers, or toting sacks of gravel. But all stopped labor to watch the three harnessed men. Big Foot threw back his head, neighed like a horse and stamped his foot.

"These drovers better look out," he threatened. "They're used to handling tame donkeys, not wild hosses. Me—I'm a stud stallion from way back."

"Reckon you're a horse, all right," sallied Acklin. "Your ears ain't long enough to be a donkey."

Captain Gomez, looking back, gestured helplessly again. He had intended to humiliate these three prisoners, to curb their high spirits. He had expected the other Texians to be impressed by this demonstration of his authority and his firmness, and to be more docile themselves. Instead, the prisoners seemed to think this was the biggest joke yet. The three harnessed men were neither ashamed nor subdued. Off they went, the first load pulled by the largest man— the hombre his companions called Big Foot— actually cavorting like a frisky colt. Gomez sighed. Never in his twelve years of army experience had he faced such a responsibility as this! Why couldn't some other officer have drawn this assignment?

He brooded darkly over just when and how he had allowed them to get out of hand. There'd been no trouble with them, at first. They had reached Perote dog-tired and resigned to accepting any orders. He had been reluctant to order them out of their cells to begin work, fearing that they couldn't endure hard labor.

Now look at them. Such prisoners there'd never been before and never would be again. Such queer customs! Their military salutes, for instance—pressing right thumb to the nose and wriggling the fingers. Why not simply touch the forehead with the right palm? Gomez was glad the Mexican army observed a more dignified gesture.

And their religious ceremonies! The captain had been roused from his sleep only two nights before; his frightened guards had reported that the Texians had gone berserk. Reaching the prison after midnight, Gomez found forty or fifty prisoners singing at the tops of their voices. Since he couldn't understand their chanting, Gomez couldn't deny the religious nature of their songs. Certainly, though, he'd never heard such racket in his own worship. Further investigation revealed a concoction of *veno mescal*, asses' milk, thirty dozen eggs and a large loaf of sugar. The captain was horrified. How had such items been smuggled into his prison? He finally found out. One or two gringos had money, the copper-haired one especially. They'd persuaded two guards to procure the materials needed for their festival punch. For a religious ritual—Captain Gomez supposed the prisoners were entitled to bless their own saints in their own way. Truly, though, these Texians were strange people.

Most difficult to handle, too. The three most consistent troublemakers pulled their carts dutifully; Gomez saw to it. Oh, the foolishness continued —the big one kept neighing, the copper-haired one kicked out at his amigo, the lame *Senor* Thompson. That one, brooded Gomez, was a drain on the prison budget. The wound in his leg refused to heal. Any hombre so afflicted could not be made to work, of course. *Senor* Thompson spent every day reclining on his elbows while his companions toiled. Were supposed to toil, that was. Gomez could not say that any of them did a respectable day's work. He couldn't finish the roadbed this spring if he had a thousand such men.

Gomez sighed. *Caramba*, what was a *capitan* to do?

But finally Big Foot, Joel and Sam tired of showing off. These carts were heavy; by noon the harnessed trio showed signs of fatigue. Captain Gomez was tempted to relent, but held out. These three seemed to be ringleaders in all the frolicking. Tame them and he might have a docile crew who would get the work done.

The prisoners were fed at noontime when doing roadwork; Gomez insisted on it. *Tortillas, frijoles, tamales*—the Texians ate as well as the garrison of Molina del Ray. Bill Thompson, the disabled hombre, showed as much appetite as the working men.

"Dang it, Bill," complained Big Foot, "you ain't able to work but you sure can eat."

Thompson grinned and confessed to having gained five pounds since leaving San Luis Potosi.

"Sure," he said, "five whole pounds. First weight I've put on in ten years."

His lank frame could stand it and Wallace said so. Thompson noticed Gomez watching them and shifted his bandaged leg gingerly. "Get on back to your hauling," he said loftily. "My amigo, the *capitan*, doesn't like me chinning with his workers."

Wallace grunted and trudged on with his cart.

Joel was dog-tired when Gomez finally gave the signal to quit.

"I don't know how long I can take this," he groaned to Sam.

"We can stand it," said Sam. "We got to. But we were sure danged fools to let ourselves in for it."

Joel nodded. Prisoners plotting escape should have known better than to attract attention to themselves. Now, Captain Pedro Gomez watched carefully every move Joel, Sam and

Big Foot made. It didn't matter so much about Wallace, for the big Virginian wasn't included in their plan.

Walker's scheme involved only three others— Joel, Ed Palmer and the supposedly lame Thompson. When they were stripped of their harness, Sam and Joel made a show of helping Bill back to the prison. Thompson pretended to be unable to make the steep incline without assistance. The guards by now were used to this display of solicitude for the injured man. Even Captain Gomez didn't suspect anything out of the way. The heavy-set captain stood at the gates, counting in the prisoners. Fearing what would happen to him if any of the Texians got away, he declined to trust this responsibility to a subordinate. Not until he was sure all were in the courtyard could he relax with his beer or *mescal.*

In they straggled, not as briskly as Gomez would have liked, and certainly not as orderly. But the important thing was that they filed by him, even the two hombres helping their compadre along. This trio brought up the rear, of course. The path was steep; it was a shame that *Senor* Thompson must travel it at least twice each day.

Joel noticed that Captain Gomez walked away before the gates were actually closed on Walker, Thompson and himself. Nor did Gomez or the guards see anything wrong with Palmer waiting just inside the prison wall. Palmer spelled off Walker as one of Thompson's supports.

In the privacy of their cell Sam reflected that things had gone well another day.

"I reckon, young 'un, we can make our break anytime, now."

Joel nodded. It seemed so to him.

They'd decided that the third afternoon of the work week was the best time. Certainly there was little point in trying to escape from their weekend prison, Perote. This grim fortress stood in a valley seven thousand feet above the sea. It was a triangle surrounded by a moat and *chevaux de frise* with a projecting bastion at each corner. The dry moat was twenty feet deep and two hundred feet wide. The most vicious convicts and criminals in Mexico were held there, and vigilance never relaxed for an instant.

Molino del Ray was softer. There was no deep encircling moat, no immediate mountainous terrain. Brushy cover, yes, and shallow but concealing arroyos. A Wednesday evening should be best. If everything had gone well the first two days, their guards would be almost relaxed by then. On Mondays and Fridays the Mexican soldiers were very tense about the responsibility of moving the Texians between Perote and Molina del Ray. So Wednesday it would be. Which Wednesday?

"Let's make it tomorrow," Sam said. "This pigeon's ready."

Joel nodded. Ready—he was more than ready. He lay back on his bunk and tried to imagine what it would be like to be free again, to be dividing his time between his land on the Medina and trapping ladinos. For Joel meant to do that, if and when he returned to Texas. He didn't tell Sam so, but he was through as a ranger. He'd fight again if another invasion came, but he'd had all of the regular service he wanted. Sure, the rangers were a great outfit and Jack Hays the best leader and friend a man could have. But there was more to be gotten out of life than chasing after human quarries. And next time, mused Joel, he'd be dead certain that any army he joined was a regular military unit. He'd sure do like Hays, turn back on his superior's say-so. Alexander Somervell had been dead right about refusing to lead his troops across the Rio Grande. Few other prisoners would admit that; not even now. Most of the Texians still clung to the notion that they'd almost won at Mier and had been chumps to give up. Sam still claimed so, and McCulloch. Both lived only to get away and take up warfare where they had left off. They would get away, too; Joel was sure of it. They were fighting men almost beyond belief. Joel Howard wasn't. Let the other rangers argue that he'd learned to handle five-shooters better than his teacher; Joel knew it wasn't so. He could shoot quicker than Walker, yes, and almost as straight. But Sam had a burning drive inside him that Joel didn't. Sam was a fighter, first, last and always. Joel wasn't. He knew it now and wondered why he had ever fancied himself as such, even for a few months.

He wanted roots, deep roots. He wanted to drive bunches of cattle to market and buy more land against the time when men couldn't trap ladinos where and when they pleased. That day was coming, as sure as sin. He wanted to build more than an adequate cabin—a hacienda, no less, with thick stone and stucco walls, with *acequias* to water fields, with docile sheep and goats to furnish wool, mutton, milk and cheese. There were a dozen ranchos to give him ideas. The Garza spread wasn't the only one he'd admired.

His first business, though, was to find out about Consuela. What if she had yielded to pressure and mated with Manuel Canales! That thought had ruined many a night's rest for him and wasn't through plaguing him by any means. He'd never rest until he found out. And all these other plans had to wait until he did know.

The next afternoon—just the thought of it made Joel shiver. They had gone over their plans until every man knew them by heart. Make the break together, then separate. It was a long way back to the Rio Grande. Just how any fugitive Texian could manage it defied Joel's imagination, or Sam's. But the man going it alone would have a better chance than any bunch.

"Sam?"

Walker turned over on his side.

"How about chips?" asked Joel. "Got any?"

"Lordee, no," Sam grunted.

Joel unbuttoned his shirt. The Mexicans had showed no curiosity about his money belt; he still had two hundred dollars in United States gold. He'd divvy equally with Sam, Thompson and Palmer. American gold might not benefit them in reaching the border, but it wouldn't hurt. Somewhere and somehow a man had to acquire a horse or mule.

Chapter Seventeen

The sun had already set, but daylight still held. *Capitan* Gomez stood at the gates counting the prisoners. Most of them spoke cheerfully as they passed him. All day the Texians had behaved pleasingly, for while only the four concerned knew exactly what the escape plan was, the others knew something was in the wind. The pudgy captain beamed as his charges filed past. Now, he was thinking, they were behaving like dutiful prisoners should. Here came the lame hombre, helped along by his two compadres. Gomez sighed. It seemed to him that *Senor* Thompson's leg should be healing.

All inside, the *capitan* observed, but the lagging trio. Gomez turned away. The four guards could be trusted to close the gate. Whistling contentedly, the *capitan* walked toward his quarters. Now a drink of tequila to wash the dust out of his mouth and he would feel like a different man.

Behind him, Bill Thompson suddenly lurched clear of Sam and fell sprawling. Immediately, Walker and Joel were all concern. Out came Ed Palmer to help them raise up the injured man. The guards showed solicitude themselves. Two even lowered their *escopetas*. The sergeant inquired if he could be of any help.

"Sure," snapped Sam Walker suddenly, freeing Thompson to launch his attack. He snatched the *escopeta* from the unsuspecting soldier and swung it as a club. Then, without looking to see if his companions had been as successful, he broke and ran. So they had planned it—every man for himself after the first blow.

Joel's designated quarry fell back a step, brought up his musket. Joel kicked away the weapon, then dived into his adversary, swinging up his knee. This had to be a strike-and-run maneuver, no time for clinching or sparring. His man staggered and Joel aimed a savage kick at his head. Then he scooped up the *escopeta* and fled. He was right on Walker's heels, tearing down the steep trail.

He heard heavy breathing right behind him and risked a look backward. There came Bill Thompson, the supposedly lame man. Joel couldn't help chuckling. For a man who couldn't walk, Bill was certainly holding a fast pace.

Had Palmer gotten away? Joel couldn't tell. Nor did he look back to see. Ahead of him Walker bolted into a shallow arroyo as musket fire came from the prison. Joel had chosen a different route. He crossed the unfinished roadbed and tore headlong into the thick brush. Thorns tore at his garments and scratched his flesh but he crashed ahead. He heard bugles behind him and more gunfire. But now no pursuers could overtake him afoot and he doubted that dragoons could follow his trail through twisting arroyos. Not immediately anyhow. And he meant to be many miles away from Molina del Ray by sunup. He'd run as long as his wind held, then walk and trot.

He recovered considerable distance by daylight, eight or ten miles at least. But he knew such a distance was nothing to dragoons scouring the country and collecting reports of any strange men that might be sighted. Joel crept into a brush tangle to rest. Thirst plagued him worse than hunger; he hadn't found any running stream or waterhole during the night. Water would be his biggest worry from here on. He meant to circle west of the main *reals*. From what little he knew about Mexico, he'd eventually find his way into the province of Coahuila. It was arid land from all he'd heard; only a desperate man would try to cross it afoot without a pack.

He examined the *escopeta* seized from the surprised guard. It was a poor weapon; one sight along its barrel showed why Texians got the best of running battles. It held only a single charge, too. Joel grimaced. One bullet—he'd better not waste it.

He stretched out, using leafy twigs to cover his

face from insects. He'd worry about food and drink later. About all he could think about now was that he'd gotten away from his Mexican jailers. Again each day held its own significance and promise. It was up to him to see that those days stretched on and on.

A needy man could devise ways to get food. Rattlesnake flesh was edible, even tasteful. Cactus pods yielded bitter but nourishing juice. Carefully he hoarded the *escopeta*'s charge. He used the gun as a club to kill rattlers and an armadillo. He drank blood as well as cactus juice. He used his tattered shirt as a seine to catch a mess of perch in a mountain creek. And, five days from Molina del Ray, he found a lonely *jacal* to raid.

First he studied the cabin carefully, watching the peon family from thick cover. A humble farmer with a handful of sheep and a rocky patch to till, a squat busy woman pounding corncakes, a bright-eyed child without a stitch of clothing— Joel had no intention of harming them. He'd risk the subsequent hue and cry when the peon reported that a wild gringo had stripped his *jacal*. He hated to rod them, but that couldn't be helped; Joel had to have a donkey, a serape, some of the ground corn, a gourd and a knife. He waited until sundown, then stole to the *jacal*'s door. The frightened family lined up against the wall as he waved the *escopeta*. Joel took what he needed, left a twenty dollar gold piece, rode off.

The donkey proved less use than he had expected. If Joel rode, he had to hold his long legs doubled. Mostly he walked, leading the docile beast bchind. But the water gourd, serape, sombrero, knife, huaraches and corn were lifesavers. Also Joel had used the peon's shears to whack off most of his hair, and soot from the *jacal*'s chimney to turn his head black. Any alarm sent out from Perote had surely mentioned that one of the gringo fugitives boasted coppery hair.

Two nights later he raided another startled family. This time he carried a shirt, pantaloons which lacked inches of reaching his ankles, more corn, another water gourd, a small scythe and two blankets. He was acquiring quite a pack for his donkey now. The next night he killed a docile ewe with the scythe and gorged on roasted mutton.

These were isolated pueblos he circled around. He was never challenged nor pursued. Blackened by the sun, and with his stained beard and hair, he might have passed for a native except for his height and blue eyes. His next raid produced a few native coins and he ventured into a pueblo to buy chili, more charges for the *escopeta* and a better-fitting sombrero. Hunched under his serape, muttering only

Spanish phrases, he attracted little attention. He took to traveling in daylight, also, presenting a stooped, shambling figure on the narrow roads. Ashes rubbed into his beard and hair made him appear an old man. Who bothered about such a nondescript, aged pilgrim, especially when a soiled blanket covered the *escopeta*?

The miles came slowly, painfully. But each one brought him nearer to the Rio Grande. Finally he plodded to within sight of Guerrero.

Chapter Eighteen

Guerrero! Here he'd come before, and as a conqueror, not a fugitive uneasy about his disguise. Joel even remembered the date he'd crossed the shallow ford with Hays' rangers to demand an indemnity of five thousand dollars. It was December 18; for on the following day General Alexander Somervell's orders had touched off the fireworks. There was small chance Joel would ever forget Guerrero and what had started less than three miles downstream.

The pueblo was busier now than on his previous visit. The Mexican flag flew proudly in the plaza. Clusters of jauntily dressed dragoons stood around the square. Joel hunched low in his serape and pulled his straw sombrero down over his eyes. He led his donkey off onto a side street, circling around the plaza. He hadn't expected to find so many soldiers in the border town. But he'd seen it deserted because of the Texian invasion; for all he knew this could be Guerrero's normal pattern.

Probably he shouldn't have ventured into this pueblo at all, but he'd been leery of crossing the Rio Grande anywhere else. From all he'd heard, the stream was not to be trusted anywhere except at regular crossing points. Quicksands and under-tows made the channel almost impossible for a man to swim. And, of course, a small, aged donkey would help a man little against a strong treacherous current.

Guerrero's natural ford had accounted for the town's location, as the convenience of crossing had established the site of Laredo. But Joel abandoned any idea of wading across so near the presidio. It might not occur to any dragoon to challenge a stooped old man and his unpretentious beast, but Joel was afraid to risk it. He'd walk downstream until he found a skiff he could appropriate and cross the river in the dark.

Jacals were scattered along the shallow bluff and he saw a number of small boats tied up to crude stone landings. He pulled his donkey back into the brush to wait for sundown. The placid animal munched grass contentedly, to Joel's envy. He wished he could be as calm and as easily satisfied.

Dusk seemed a long time coming and Joel waited longer than that—waited until candles were snuffed out in the adobe huts along the river. Then he patted the donkey and said, "*vaya con Dios, amigo.*" In high spirits, he stole toward the river bank. If all went well, he'd be walking on Texas soil the next day. Just let him get one glimpse of the Lone Star flag and he'd show his feeling with the loudest yell ever heard north of the Rio Grande.

He had spotted three skiffs hitched to a small stone wharf before sundown. He found them easily enough, and—he thought—without making any tell-tale noises. He tested their rawhide fastenings, chose one to unknot. Struggling with its complicated hitch, he didn't hear the Mexican approaching. The hombre's sharp question hit him like a slap in the face.

"*Quien es?*"

Joel raised up. "*Caramba!*" roared the Mexican. A knife glinted in the dark; Joel threw up his *escopeta*. The musket snapped and that was all. By then his assailant was on him; Joel cursed and used the *escopeta* to parry the knife thrust. He leaped out of the bobbing boat to get better footing, for this indignant hombre meant business. He was also calling for help at the top of his voice. Joel dodged a vicious swipe and charged in under the Mexican's thrust. He locked the hombre's knife arm in a desperate clutch and tried to hurl his adversary into the water. But this was no average-sized Mexican; Joel couldn't spin him off. Meanwhile, shouts came from the *jacals* above and down scrambled two other natives. Joel had his man by the throat when the reinforcements attacked. One of them struck with some sort of a mallet. Joel wavered on his feet and then was buried under their collective weights. He lay, half-senseless, while the Mexicans chattered excitedly. Down the shallow bluff waddled a woman carrying a candle. Its glare struck Joel squarely in the face and the natives saw through his disguise immediately. *Caramba*, a gringo! Now a cluster of natives, old and young, male and female, chattered excitedly about their captive. Off scurried a *muchacho* to fetch the commandant of the garrison. Joel, shaking off his grogginess, tried to break free. The last thing he wanted was to be questioned by a Mexican officer.

The same three hombres subdued him again. As he subsided, Joel heard one of the onlookers marvel at the strength of so old a man. He went limp in their clutches, pretending that all of his fight was gone. Let them relax for an instant, just one instant. Let him get into the river and he'd take his chances on the quicksands and current.

But his captors didn't fall for the ruse. Cursing, jabbering, they held him until a half-dozen soldiers came hurrying to the wharf. One of them spoke with authority. As he came closer Joel saw the glitter of his uniform. Then he saw the officer's features in the candle's flickering gleam and this time he wrested free of the encircling arms. The sight of that face gave him the strength to break bands of steel. Manuel Canales! The name was a babble from

Joel's lips as he crashed into the nearby brush.

Behind him came a hubbub of excited talk and scurrying motion. Had Canales recognized him, too? Joel shook his head; he was not sure. But Canales knew that the fleeing man was a gringo. The Mexicans had noticed Joel's blue eyes. Did Canales know about the escape from Perote? It didn't matter, for Canales was organizing a large-scale pursuit anyhow. How many men were tearing into the brush after the gringo? Dozens, anyhow; at least, the fleeing man was sure there were that many. He'd only run a little way before he realized his weakness. He was short of wind, woefully so. He felt hollow all the way to his toes. There was no reason to think he could outrun even the hombres pursuing him afoot, much less the mounted dragoons.

For he heard horsemen now, mounted men flailing the brush with their sabers. Joel flung himself face down in a shallow wash. His only hope was that they'd pass by him. He didn't dare leave the thickets for open prairie. The moonlight was alarmingly bright and he knew these dragoons would shoot him down on sight.

He eluded the first wave of pursuers and desperately sought another hiding place. Maybe the pueblo offered his best bet, after all. He crouched against a *jacal* to avoid another party of lancers.

Not only the soldiers were out in full strength, but almost all of Guerrero's entire populace. A shrill feminine voice spread the alarm as Joel darted off to another *jacal.* Her cry set off another bedlam. A dozen horsemen rode within several paces of the wanted man as he crouched behind a stone cistern. Barking dogs added to the pande-monium. Several of the excited beasts caught the gringo's scent and were yapping around him before he realized this latest menace. He vaulted up on a rooftop and threw himself flat. Human eyes couldn't spot him but the damning dogs kept up with him as he leaped to another *jacal.* The dogs have found him! The hoarse shout sounded again and again. Joel groaned. There was no eluding the yapping four-legged beasts. He'd be no safer in a brush patch, either, not with these canines on his trail. He couldn't manage a leap to the next *jacal.* The chase was over; no use to doubt it.

Already dragoons were closing in around him. Joel peered cautiously over the roof's edge. They were milling around as if waiting for someone to give orders. The yapping dogs were scratching against the adobe walls, some even trying to climb up.

Here came the voice of authority—Canales. Up on the roof, he snapped. Cut the gringo down. The hated voice came closer. Joel ventured another look. Canales stood almost directly beneath him.

Joel acted in sudden instinct—and in desperation. He couldn't get away. He couldn't avoid recapture and what mercy could an escaped prisoner of Perote expect? He dived from the roof and landed squarely on Canales' shoulders. The captain collapsed and Joel gripped the Mexican's throat with both hands. The suddenness of his attack numbed every soldier there. Twenty of them could have rushed to their commandant's help in time, but didn't. They stood rooted in their tracks, eyes bulging in their sockets, until the bearded gringo tottered to his feet and faced them with a wild eerie cry of triumph.

For a long time Joel Howard lay on the dirt floor without moving. Finally he stirred, awakening to such pain as he had never before felt. A thousand hammers seemed to be pounding against his temples. His eyes couldn't focus clearly; he made out the details of his dingy cell through a shimmering haze. Finally he saw the straw mattress and crawled toward it. There, he lay face downward for another while, until raging thirst brought him to his feet. He staggered to the iron door and clung to its bar.

"*Agua,*" he croaked. "*Agua.*"

A guard finally ventured into the corridor. He

considered the prisoner a moment, then went for his sergeant. The two of them came close enough to understand Joel's hoarse pleadings. The guard brought a gourd of water and allowed Joel to drink through the bars. Unlock the door! Neither Mexican was about to do that. They were afraid of this wild-eyed Texian and didn't mind showing it.

Joel fell back on the mattress. He remembered nothing about being dragged to this prison. He recalled rising to his feet after strangling Canales. He had meant to surrender without further resis-tance but the Mexican soldiers had clubbed him with their musket butts anyhow. They'd beaten him down less than five hundred yards from the banks of the Rio Grande.

Joel groaned. From Molina del Ray's gates to Guerrero was a long way. How many miles was it—four hundred, five hundred! He had managed all of the distance except the river. He'd detoured wide around Saltillo and Monterey, around any pueblo which had seemed to have a garrison of any size. But the Rio Grande had trapped him—the Rio and a rabble and the Mexican officer who seemed to be his personal nemesis. He'd settled his personal score, but maybe it had been a fool thing to do. But he couldn't be sorry about it, not even if the price was his own life. That would be the price, too; no reason to doubt it. What else could a Mexican commandant do with a Texian who had escaped Perote and had strangled a captain, except shoot him?

He struggled to his feet and this time was strong enough to rattle the bars. *"Alimento,"* he shouted. He had learned in Salado and Perote that the noisiest prisoner got the most attention. He threatened his guard and then raged at the sergeant. Neither would bring him food but his uproar finally produced the prison commandant. He clattered something before walking off. But he must have given orders to feed the prisoner, for shortly the nervous guards brought him *tamales* and a thin sort of chocolate. The *tamales* were cold but Joel finished the last crumbs. He was still hungry. Probably, he thought, he could eat for a solid week without being fully satisfied.

He stretched out on the mattress again. His head still throbbed, but he knew now that he could endure its aching. For as long as he had to, anyhow. Surely the local commandant would not have to wait for specific instructions from Santa Anna. Wouldn't there be some sort of general order about immediate execution for the Texians who had escaped from Perote?

Joel's spirits rose as his suffering eased. He'd get out of this jail if there was any stalling around about his execution. He came off the floor. There might be such a delay, too. Weren't

Mexicans always putting everything off? Look how long they'd been held at Salado before anything was decided.

His cell had a single window. He could reach his bars by standing on his tiptoes. There was no budging them. He'd have to chip away considerable mortar first. Even then, he might not be able to wriggle out the opening, which wasn't over two feet square.

His captors had cleaned out his pockets. He still had two gold coins, but these made no impression on the hard mortar. Joel lay back on the mattress. Somehow he must get his hands on a knife or a piece of iron. He might manage it if there was time and he could lull his guards into a sense of false security. Hadn't he managed to get out of Perote and come this far? Then, in midafternoon, a small procession came down the corridor and Joel heard his sentence from Colonel Humberto Salazar, commander of the Guerrero garrison. The colonel spoke formally without bothering to have the door unlocked. *Senor* Howard would face a firing squad at sunrise. The colonel was willing to consider any requests the condemned man wished to make.

Joel nodded. This blew to smithereens his ideas about escaping. But he had expected it. The colonel and his retinue of four soldiers stood waiting patiently. Finally Salazar repeated his offer. Did the prisoner have any last request?

Joel frowned. He hadn't taken this gesture seriously. It wasn't his experience that prison commandants showed such consideration.

"What's there to ask for?" he shrugged. "I'm still hungry, that's for sure."

"You will be fed," promised the colonel. "An excellent meal, too. And your valuables, if any, will be kept for anyone you say." Salazar did not add that he had no idea how delivery could ever be arranged.

Joel shook his head. He had twenty dollars in American money. Why bother with it?

"I've a little money, that's all," he said. "If you'll see that I get enough to eat—and water to wash with and a razor—and something to drink besides water—milk or *aguardiente*—you're welcome to my money."

Colonel Salazar nodded. The prisoner would get food, drink and bath. And the money would be distributed among the guards if the *senor* had no objection.

Joel looked at this officer with more respect. *Salazar*, he decided, was a gentleman. The commandant reminded him of Governor Mexia and General Ampudia. And also Don Carlos' formal courtesy.

"That's all I can think of, Colonel. *Gracias*."

The conscientious Salazar was not satisfied. "Among our people it is customary for a priest to hear a man's last confessions. Is there anything that can be done for you in that regard, *senor*?"

Joel shook his head. "I wish there were," he said. And he meant it. For the colonel's words brought recollection of Consuela's daily prayers. She had returned from each recital full of cheerful penance and bright hope. He added, "I don't reckon I'd know what to say to a priest, or him to me."

"Father Muldoon is an exceptional padre," said Salazar. "He's well-acquainted with the customs of your people, too. I can't promise that he'll see you, but I'll ask if you wish."

"Father Muldoon!" said Joel.

"You know him?"

"Yes." How could he forget the genial Irishman he had rescued from Jared Applegate? The priest, thought Joel, would probably know what had happened to Consuela in these past months.

"Ask Father Muldoon if he will come and see me," Joel said. "If he doesn't remember me right off, remind him that I'm the gringo he met at a *baille* in Agua Dulce."

"It shall be done," Colonel Salazar promised.

Chapter Nineteen

It wasn't necessary to remind Father Muldoon of his prior meeting with Joel Howard. The priest quickly agreed to see the prisoner as soon as his study was empty of visitors. Guerrero was the seat of the padre's big parish. Here he lived in comfortable quarters with a wrinkled *criedo* to attend his wants.

The guard brought him to Joel's cell immediately. Father Muldoon greeted Joel through the bars, then asked to be let in.

"Oh, nonsense," the priest said, as the guard hesitated. "Unlock the door at once. *Senor* Howard and I are old friends and we have much to talk about."

The guard opened the door without further delay. Father Muldoon usually got his way in Guerrero.

"It's good of you to come, Father," Joel said awkwardly. "I was afraid you wouldn't."

"And why shouldn't I?"

Joel shrugged his shoulders. "I'm a dangerous hombre. I got out of Perote with a whole skin, and killed a captain. From choice, too, not because I had to."

"I heard about Captain Canales' death," the

priest said slowly. "My informants said that a gringo circled back and attacked Canales like a madman. It didn't occur to me it was you, Joel. I suppose it should have."

"I saw my chance," Joel said grimly, "and I took it. I can't be sorry for it, either, Father. Canales tried to have me killed."

"I know," nodded the Irishman. "You had unusual provocation." The padre hesitated. "Have you heard about Consuela?"

"Just what Canales told me at Mier. She got back to Agua Dulce safely." Joel heaved a deep sigh. "Canales boasted that she would marry him when this fight was over. That could be another reason that I had—to—"

"She would never have married him," Father Muldoon said firmly. "Don Carlos proposed it, yes. But Consuela threatened to enter a convent first. She has loved you, my son."

"Then why did she skip back home?"

The priest studied the toes of his sandals a moment. Would it make dying any easier for this rawboned young man if he knew the truth. Father Muldoon decided it would.

"She didn't return of her own free will, my son. Canales sent two men to your cabin—the two men who tried to make sport with me at Agua Dulce."

"Applegate? Boulain?"

"Yes. They kidnapped Consuela and brought

215

her back. She vows to rejoin you if the chance ever comes."

Joel trembled. "And I'm cooped up here," he said bitterly. "Due to be shot at daylight."

"Yes, I know. Colonel Salazar told me. He can't do anything else, Joel. Every local commandant has orders direct from Santa Anna to execute any Texian prisoner who is recaptured."

"Oh, I know that," Joel said quickly. "Colonel Salazar has been—well, he's a gentleman. That's the only way I know to put it."

Father Muldoon had to smile. "He said the same about you—and other Texians. And I must add that nobody appears grieved about what happened to Captain Canales. There are many Mexicans, Joel, who shudder at the mention of Mier."

"I reckon," nodded Joel. "And some of us Texians," he added ruefully, "wish to hell we hadn't been so rambunctious." He sighed. "I'm sure glad to learn Consuela never thought twice about marrying Canales. I reckon she oughta marry somebody. I want her to—especially now—so—"

"So your child will have a name and a father?"

Joel's eyes flashed. "Don't talk like that, Father. Any child born to Consuela has a name. A father, too. I know, we never had any sort of a ceremony. We didn't have the chance. That's what brought out this business about Woll sashaying in to Texas. Consuela told me about it when we were talking about going back to Agua Dulce and asking you to marry us right. I wasn't about to do it because I didn't want to kill any more of Don Carlos' vaqueros. I'd shot three of 'em already, or thought I had. Then—"

"Let me have the whole story," suggested the priest. "From the very beginning. This way, I'm only getting confused."

Joel gave an account of his elopement and their brief life on the Medina. He added his enlistment with the rangers, the march to Guerrero, the breakup of Somervell's force, the assault on Mier.

Father Muldoon's eyes twinkled. "How did Consuela fare in a cabin?"

"Not so good, at first," Joel said truthfully. "But she perked up. She showed it can be done, Father. Mexicans and *Yanquis* can live together." He grinned. "Oh, we had our spats, Father. Usually she got the best of 'em. She can talk rings around me. She's spoiled and I'm as stubborn as an old mule—but we were happy. Awfully happy. Happier than I ever thought I could be."

"And the difference in faith didn't create dissension?"

"Golly, no. I don't reckon Consuela would give in to anybody about that." Joel shook his shaggy head. "I never saw anything like that girl, Father. We no sooner got to the Medina than she rigged up her own place to pray." His grin came again. "I worked on the sly and built her a little chapel. Trimmed the heart of a cedar into a right pretty cross, too. She got up at daylight and pattered barefoot to her prayers." He hesitated. "I wasn't sure of what she did or said there, but I was sort of proud of her for it."

"I understand," Father Muldoon said gently. His eyes studied Joel thoughtfully, his forehead wrinkling. Then Father Muldoon called for the guard. "I'll be back tonight," he told Joel. "You'll need me then—from midnight on. I'm sure Colonel Salazar will make you as comfortable as he can."

Two guards brought in a small tub of warm water, soap, a razor and rough toweling. Joel stripped off his ragged garments and scrubbed himself vigorously. He attacked his whiskers with the razor. The guards returned to his cell before he had finished. They had new garments, gray homespun shirt and trousers. The latter were too big in the waist but Joel tore off a strip of his old shirt to keep them up. Next came food and wine, but the guards refused to unlock the cell door until Joel had handed the razor through the bars. These prison attendants meant to be kind, but they were also wary.

The meal was lavish—chicken, browned rice,

beans, avocado, strong-smelling cheese. Joel ate until he was stuffed. He drank a full bottle of wine, too, then was offered *aguardiente.*

"I'll try it," he said sheepishly, "but I'm full to the gills already."

He lay back on his elbows while most of his unruly hair was snipped off. By then it was pitch-black outside his cell—about nine o'clock, he guessed. He didn't expect Father Muldoon until midnight. He stretched out on his side as the cell door clanged shut. This Salazar, he mused, had certainly put on the big dog for him. He'd never eaten such a meal in his life and his cleanliness was nothing short of thrilling. He found it easy to fall asleep.

He came awake when the key turned in his cell. Father Muldoon was being admitted.

"Is it all right to leave you alone, Father?" the soldier asked.

"Quite all right, Ricardo," said the Irishman. "And quite customary, too."

Off trudged the guard. Father Muldoon sat by Joel on the straw mattress.

"How do you feel now, Joel? Colonel Salazar told me what had been done for you."

"Fine, Father. Never ate so much in my life. Went for the brandy, too."

"You are prepared for daylight?"

"Shucks, no. Reckon no man is ever really ready for it. Especially not now."

"What do you mean?"

"What you told me about Consuela."

"You can pray for her, my son."

"I sure will. I already have. But I want you to pray, too, Father. I reckon you can get a hearing where I can't."

"No, Joel," the priest said gently. "Only you can be heard. I offer so many prayers that one more doesn't have much effect. But you—I know our God will glory in your concern for the happiness of others. So pray, Joel. Kneel with me."

Joel obeyed. He felt awkward trying to imitate the padre's example.

"Pray aloud, Joel," whispered Father Muldoon. "Convince the guards that you intend to pray a long time. Let them get sleepy and forget about us. For you are getting out of here, Joel. I'll help you escape, on one condition."

"I'll do anything, Father," Joel whispered back. "Just name it."

"Do you remember the hut where I dressed your bruises after your fight with Applegate?"

"I sure do."

"Promise me you'll wait for me there. That you won't try to see Consuela until I have followed you to Agua Dulce."

"Why, Father?"

"I have my good reasons, Joel. You must trust me."

"I do that Father. I won't try to see her."

"Or let anyone see you. There must be no more violence."

"Yes, sir."

"Now, Joel, listen carefully. Wait until the guards are asleep. Then you take my frock and cover yourself the best you can. Imitate me and call the guard. He'll be sleepy-eyed and might not see who it is in the dark. Don't strike him down unless you have to. If you can get out without a hue and cry, you'll have several hours' start."

Joel's heart leaped. Given a start, allowed to get across the river!

"But what about you, Father?"

"I'll be all right. You can take my cord and tie my hands. The rags of your old clothes will do for a gag. Nobody will doubt that you over- came me and got away."

"But—"

"No buts," Father Muldoon said firmly. "It's the only way, my son. And you must keep your word about waiting for me at my *jacal*."

Joel nodded.

"Once across the river," continued the priest, "you can manage afoot. Let no one see you. To steal or buy a horse would only put out an alarm. Do you promise, Joel?"

"I do."

"All right. Let us pray together."

They waited for what seemed to Joel to be hours. Finally Muldoon whispered they could act. He pulled off his cassock and Joel slipped it over his shoulders. He tied the Irishman's hands with a cord and knotted his discarded trousers about the priest's mouth. Then he clanged softly on the bars to get the guard's attention. He crouched as the soldier came stumbling down the corridor.

"The prisoner sleeps," Joel said gruffly. "He has made his peace with God."

The guard mumbled something and opened the door. Joel moved cautiously down the corridor, leaving the soldier to struggle with the lock. He walked past a sleeping guard and out into the clear, crisp night.

Chapter Twenty

For a while Father Muldoon lay as if actually unable to do anything about his bonds. He kept thinking that a guard might decide to check on the prisoner, and the padre wanted a convincing show. But as minutes ticked on, he loosened the knots until he could lie comfortably on the straw mattress. There he slept until almost dawn. Awakening, he called the guard immediately, as if he had just managed to get loose.

The guard came stumbling down the hall, cursing a gringo dog who yelled out at so early an hour. He could hardly believe his own eyes when he saw Father Muldoon shaking the bars and demanding to be let out.

"Merciful Saints!" gasped the soldier, fumbling for his keys. "What happened, Father?"

"What does it look like?" demanded the Irishman, pretending to be quite peeved. "*Senor* Howard overpowered me and took my clothes. You let him out, mistaking him for me. And that was almost five hours ago. There's little doubt where he is now—across the river."

The guard trembled as he opened the door. "They will blame me," he moaned. "I will get thirty lashes anyhow."

"Not if I can help it. The fault was mine. I

shouldn't have insisted you leave me alone with such a dangerous man. You didn't want to do it."

"So I didn't," the soldier said eagerly. "I really didn't, Father. Will you tell Colonel Salazar that?"

"I certainly will. Take me to him."

"So early, Father? To wake him now—that would only put him in a worse humor."

The Irishman smiled. He knew why Humberto Salazar did not want to be roused so early. The colonel usually drank and gambled until midnight.

"I'll rouse him out," Father Muldoon said. *"Senor* Howard must be caught if possible. Once across the river—with a horse under him—he is gone."

Colonel Salazar finally bellowed in answer to the pounding on his door. Father Muldoon heard loud groans and profane mutterings as the sleepy man fumbled for his clothes. The colonel flung open the door and demanded why he had been disturbed. His manner changed when he saw the priest.

"Why, Father Muldoon! What in the world brings you here?" The colonel then glared at the unhappy guard. "And what have you done wrong now?"

"He has done nothing," Muldoon said quickly. "If anyone is to blame, it is myself. Let us in and I will tell you about it."

224

Colonel Salazar came quickly awake with the announcement of Joel's escape. The officer's impatience showed long before Father Muldoon finished his account. Salazar, apologizing for his abruptness, dashed out of his quarters and set dragoons to stirring about. The Irishman, still pretending chagrin and concern, withdrew to his room as soon as he could. He was tired, he hadn't slept too soundly on the straw mattress. Nor long enough. But he was quite pleased with himself as he stretched out on his comfortable bed and directed his *criedo* to bar all visitors. There was no doubt that Joel had reached safety across the river.

Why was he so smug about what he had done? Father Muldoon asked himself that the next morning as he rode his mule toward Agua Dulce. What justification was there for a man of God interfering with civil justice? Joel Howard had broken one of the Commandments. Regardless of his provocation, he had taken human life. Was a priest justified in befriending a killer under any circumstances? Was it a priest's mission to put aside his regular duties and ride almost a hundred miles to remonstrate with a bitter grandfather? The priest sighed. Such performances would certainly shock his superiors. He might even be stripped of his cloth if the truth became known.

But since when had Andrew Muldoon informed

his superiors about the details of his doings? Not since the early 1820's, anyhow. For two-score years he had functioned with practically no interference from any church authority and even less help. The priest smiled as he recalled his first assignment to the Texas settlements. When was it—1824 or 1825? Time had a way of slipping by, and man a way of forgetting. Stephen F. Austin had just secured ratification of his contract to settle immigrants from the United States on the Brazos River. Actually the colonies were already launched; Austin's original grant had come from the King of Spain, shortly before the overthrow of the monarchy in Mexico. Revolution had held up and complicated full recognition of his settlers as Mexican citizens. Austin himself had delivered Father Muldoon's instructions from the Bishop of Monclava. Several hundred colonists had been without any sort of unction for two years. All had agreed to conform with Mexican laws about the Catholic faith.

It was 1825—March, 1825. Father Muldoon had reached San Felipe de Austin about sundown and had performed his first mass wedding ceremony that night, uniting no less than twenty couples in holy matrimony.

From 1825 to 1836—for over eleven years Father Muldoon had served all of Texas as well as his parish in Tamaulipas. Often he'd mused upon his impossible assignment. As a mere priest he had a bigger domain than any bishop. The Texas victory at San Jacinto had enabled the immigrants to drop their Catholic pretenses. Except some hadn't been pretending. Others had been actually converted. Did a priest's responsibilities cease because of a battle? Muldoon didn't think so.

On he plodded, absorbed with his recollections and his musings. There was no doubt about the political trend of Texas, or even of the Rio Grande country. Father Muldoon thought back to Manuel Mier y Teran, the shrewdest Mexican statesman of his experience. Teran had foreseen that the people from the United States would dominate Texas. He had wanted to counteract their spreading influence by counter-colonization of Mexican families along the Brazos and Colorado Rivers. That failing, he had encouraged European immigrants. He'd taken his own life in 1832 because of his failure to accomplish his dream.

The tide from across the Sabine could not be stopped. Father Muldoon had seen them come on and on. The Brazos first, then the Colorado. Their march had halted for a while before the Medina. The average settler balked at the dry expanse of brushy waste. But not all Americans. Ewen Cameron's cowboys had come riding into the *brasada*. Others would follow.

The gringo was the stronger man in this new country. He saw its opportunities more clearly. He adapted himself better to its new measurements. This could never be a New Spain, no doubt of that, and Father Muldoon did not like to visualize it as a sort of New United States, either. Let it be a fusion of some things handed on from both civilizations, but different, too.

That night Father Muldoon stopped at the pueblo of San Carlos. He hoped Joel Howard would not grow too impatient, but a priest owed overdue services wherever he stopped. The same was true at Santo Marion, and at the rancho of Carlos Esquival. Infants to baptize, confessions to hear, betrothals to bless—the Irishman always traveled slowly. He reached Agua Dulce three days later.

He put his conference with Don Carlos ahead of any visits to the *jacals*, which pleased the *proprietor.*

"Usually," said Garza, "you have no time for me until you are finished with everyone else."

"This time it is different. I'm here to see you."

"And what grievous sin have I committed? I know nothing else would prompt such attention."

"You have committed no sin. No unusual one, anyhow."

"And what do you mean by that?"

"I can't tell you in a single breath," said the

priest, "nor with such a dry, rasping throat. A swallow of port might get me started."

"Of course," apologized Don Carlos, clapping his hands for a servant. "A thousand pardons."

A few minutes later the Irishman declared himself ready for serious talk.

"How is Consuela?"

The patron's face darkened. "She is doing as well as could be expected." He stared at the slender glass goblet. "Except there seems little hope for her future."

"What do you mean?"

"She refuses to even consider marriage to anyone else. The silly child insists that she still loves the gringo. She vows that she will go into a convent if I try to force her into any marriage."

"Do you blame her?"

"Do I blame her!" snapped Garza. "Mother of God, what kind of talk is that! She has one offer of honorable marriage—with Manuel Canales. And if not that, then—"

"He is dead. Killed last week in Guerrero."

"Dead!" Don Carlos hurriedly crossed himself. "Tell me about it." He listened, then said: "There is Ramon Esquival. There could be others if the silly girl would admit the truth about her tragic experience. But she insists that she lived happily with this—this cowboy. What can be done about folly like that?"

"Believe her," the priest said calmly. "I'm sure she speaks the truth."

Don Carlos glared at the padre. "Has she sent you any message? Has she asked your intervention?"

"No."

"Then spare yourself the effort," snapped the *proprietor.* "For once in her life Consuela will obey me. Or enter a convent if she must. One far away from here."

"And who would suffer the most from that? What would you gain for Agua Dulce? What would happen then to this great estate and your noble line?"

"Bah!" said Don Carlos. "You talk nonsense." He leaped to his feet. "What am I to do?" he roared. "Accept this *Yanqui* adventurer as a son-in-law? Don't get me disgusted with you, Father."

"Go ahead. I am disgusted with you already."

"Such a priest," Garza said bitterly, "there never was before and never will be again. Do you mean to sit there and countenance this union? Since when has our Church smiled upon such marriages?"

"It never has and it never will," the priest said promptly. "But in this new empty country the Church has considered circumstances and held out the promise of atonement. I have looked into the circumstances. There was no priest

230

available on the Medina River where this couple fled. Had there been, Consuela and Joel Howard would be so married now that not even your obstinacy could tear them apart."

"You have seen her," charged Don Carlos. "Either that or you have communicated with her."

"I have not seen her since last summer. I have not received any communication at all from her." The padre emptied his glass, then admitted that he had talked with Joel Howard. "In fact," he said, "I helped him escape to Texas. He's not far from Agua Dulce at this moment. And he's determined to get Consuela back. I think he will, too."

"I'll keep her guarded day and night," thundered Garza. "The gringo doesn't live who can slip by my vaqueros."

"This one can," Father Muldoon said calmly. "Apparently, amigo, you don't appreciate what Texians can do with their five-shooters. A handful of men like Joel Howard came near to slaughtering Ampudia's army at Mier. The Texians numbered less than two hundred. They killed over six hundred and wounded two hundred more. Joel Howard can collect twenty or so rangers like himself and tear your rancho apart. Come out of the hoary past, Don Carlos, and face reality. This Joel Howard represents a new generation. Almost a new breed."

Don Carlos trembled, but did not deny the priest's words. Instead, the Spaniard growled, "Savages, barbarians, heretics! Is the sad history of Europe to be repeated here, and these men triumph?"

"He is none of those things, amigo."

Don Carlos almost exploded. "Merciful Saints, Father! Do you defend this man?"

"Partially," nodded the priest. "You must admit that he shows enterprise and ability. He is poor still, as you measure wealth. But already he can handle cattle better than your vaqueros, who were born to it. He knows how to sell cattle at a profit, which you don't. He can build his own cabin, kill his own food, earn money and save it. Consuela would not starve with such a man."

"Maybe that. But what faith has he? Is he even a Protestant?"

"Hardly. But don't take any holier-than-thou attitude about this young couple, Don Carlos. Neither Consuela nor Joel Howard. Did she tell you about their chapel?"

"Partially. Why?"

"And you were not impressed?"

"A little," the *proprietor* conceded reluctantly. "It shows Consuela has been reared properly."

"More than that. Your granddaughter no sooner reached the Medina than she became concerned about her soul. Pampered and spoiled as she has been, she took vines and poles and made herself a crude sanctuary. Joel Howard—this young man you deride as a heretic—took his axe and built a chapel with his own hands. He finished a crucifix out of the heart of a cedar. He did that before he even had a roof on his cabin, or learned how far his cattle had strayed. Is that the doing of a godless man? Did the first Garza to reach Agua Dulce Creek worry about a place to pray and confess before he had raised his own shelter? I doubt it."

Don Carlos stroked his beard. "Your talents are wasted," he growled. "You can outtalk the devil himself. You always could."

The Irishman's eyes twinkled. "I speak only the truth, amigo. Joel Howard and Consuela I can help attain a full and happy life. It is you I am most concerned about."

"Me?"

"Of course. What if you persist in your stubbornness? Your granddaughter will go; she will follow this gringo to the end of the earth. She needs him, but nothing like you do."

"I need him?" The *proprietor* laughed bitterly. "As I need the plague, Father."

"Who'll hold Agua Dulce for you in your declining years, then?" demanded Muldoon.

"Who threatens to take it?" countered Garza.

The priest pointed northward. "The Americans. They are already moving south of the Medina.

233

They'll reach the Nueces next. Mexico will never regain this land. You spoke of Manuel Canales. He was never the man for Agua Dulce. He proved himself a cruel man. Because of such men Mexico has lost prestige in the eyes of the world. The black bean lottery at Salado will not be soon forgotten, amigo. I am not supposed to prophesize history. But already the repercussions of Mier are being felt. The Mexican people are wearying of their own brutal dictator. The people of the United States are again conscious of their blood brothers living along the Texas rivers. Do I need remind you of what happened in 1836?" The priest paused for breath, went on:

"For six years a political faction in the United States has thwarted annexation of Texas into their union. Public opinion is rising again. Texas will join the United States, Don Carlos. So forget about these warmongers of the Rio Grande, either a Canales or a Juan Seguin or a Dick Fisher or an Ewen Cameron. Theirs was a small war. A hundred years from now it would be forgotten except for one thing—the black bean drawing. The lottery of death. Eighteen men died that day at Salado. Six hundred Mexicans gave their lives to set up their execution. Theirs was a wasted sacrifice. So would be yours, my long and good friend. There's nothing against this young man except your prejudices."

Don Carlos refilled his glass with a trembling hand.

"You go around in the guise of a priest," he complained, "but you have the forked tongue of a devil. How could there ever be reconciliation of my beliefs and my heritage with what this Joel Howard personifies?"

"There must be," shrugged Father Muldoon. "There will be. You have no choice, Don Carlos. You have a strong pride of heritage. I have heard it called an order of men. Such so-called orders of men are always changing. The man who is both wise and happy accepts that change. In your case, you should be grateful for it. You need that *Yanqui* son-in-law, Don Carlos. You need him as a buffer between you and all that you do not understand. You need him because this broad *porcion* is the Garza past, its present and its future. You can help him and he can help you. If all he is today can be embraced into what your line has been, if his rugged ways can be tempered by your ideals and your gracious example—"

The priest gestured with both hands.

"No doubt of it, then," he said softly. "The Garza *porcion* will never be broken up. The roots of the Garzas will be planted deep."

Don Carlos' head dropped to his chest. "You're always right," he confessed. "I am old. I do need a strong man—and I doubt that I could live long without Consuela."

• • •

A thousand times Joel had imagined that he heard or saw Father Muldoon coming; each time had turned out to be just another disappointment.

These days, he reflected bitterly, had been almost as taxing as his imprisonment. In Mexico, at least, he'd had company in his misery. There'd been Big Foot Wallace's irrepressible humor, Ben McCulloch's fiery spirit, Sam Walker's cool confidence in himself and his comrades, Mike Chevaille's unflagging determination. There'd been Mexican guards to torment, and cockroaches to use as playthings and a thousand yarns a day to hear—all the more interesting because one never knew the difference between truth and fantasy.

Here was physical comfort, yes. Joel had found enough in the *jacal* to eat. There was a comfortable couch and the adobe hut held a pleasant temperature day or night. But there were offsetting torments. Not only the loneliness, but, more gnawing, the waiting with Consuela not more than three miles away. The Garza hacienda of stucco and stone was in sight from morning to night. Occasionally Juan and his vaqueros rode within a hundred yards of the *huisache* thicket. Joel couldn't look out of the hut's single window without being reminded that she was close at hand—kept from him only by his promise to Father Muldoon.

But he stuck it out, and finally the priest came plodding toward the *jacal* on his gray mule. Joel had never been so happy to see anyone in his life. But the Irishman refused to divulge much about his talk with Don Carlos.

"It would take a long time," said the priest, "and I am tired of talking. I have talked too much this day, even for me. Let us be going."

"Where to?"

"Where else?" asked Father Muldoon with a smile. "To the hacienda."

"You mean—!" Joel stammered.

"Of course," nodded the priest. "The wedding ceremony mustn't be delayed another day."

Joel's eyes gleamed. Then, Don Carlos had given his consent? Father Muldoon held up his hand. Explanations could wait, he declared.

Joel strode alongside the mule. They covered a part of the distance in silence, then the Irishman decided to relieve some of Joel's anxiety. "Everything is as I hoped," Muldoon said. "And as it should be. Most of the burden of understanding will be yours, Joel. Never forget that Don Carlos is an old man. And weighed down with the prejudices of more years than he actually has. He won't accept you immediately, not wholeheartedly; he couldn't, to save his soul. But keep in mind that the stakes are high and great prizes never come easily or quickly. Agua Dulce was not organized in a day or a year. These thousands of cattle and horses and sheep didn't spring out of the ground like bursting seed. Don Carlos will try hard, but yours must be the greater effort."

"What do you mean, Father?"

"What do I mean?" the priest chuckled. "What else, my son? Look around you in every direction. Is there such a rancho on the Rio Grande or anywhere else? If so, I have never seen it. And will it be easy to become its next *patron*?"

Joel started. He scowled at the priest, then shook his head. "No," he said firmly. "I have my own land, my own start. I want Consuela, that's all."

Father Muldoon shook his head. "No, my son." He waved his arm. "All this—it's Consuela, too. That began a long time ago. It is too late to stop it now, even if it should be stopped. But no more argument, please. I have dealt with one difficult man already today. Both my strength and my patience are wearing thin."

They reached the hacienda and Father Muldoon surrendered his mule to a young *criedo* and led the way to the massive oak door. It opened before he could knock and Don Carlos stood there, a strained expression on his face, but determined to face this ordeal.

"Here he is, Don Carlos," said the priest.

"So I see," the *proprietor* said. His eyes met Joel's, then looked off. "Take him to her, Father,"

Don Carlos said softly. "She is waiting for him on the back patio. It was her idea to meet him there."

Joel trembled. The patio, of course.

Don Carlos addressed Joel without looking at him. "I deplore my manners, *senor*," he said tonelessly. "This is even more difficult than I had expected. But we will manage—the three of us. As Father Muldoon has said, we must. I beg your tolerance—and your forgiveness in advance for any difficulties I will cause."

Joel licked his lips and stared down at the floor.

"It is I who must be forgiven, Don Carlos," he managed to say. "Consuela will tell you that I always do things wrong. I don't know much— about the right way to do things. I just—" He heaved a deep sigh. "I just don't know what to say," he added helplessly.

"There is no more to be said," declared Father Muldoon. "Not now, at least. Just hurry along, lad. Consuela has waited a long time. Tomorrow will be soon enough to worry about amends to your father-in-law."

Joel moved quickly to obey. Four long strides and he had reached the corridor. Six more and he was out in the patio, and Consuela was in his arms.

Center Point Large Print
600 Brooks Road / PO Box 1
Thorndike, ME 04986-0001 USA

(207) 568-3717

US & Canada:
1 800 929-9108
www.centerpointlargeprint.com